The Lion's Den

Chronicles of a Las Vegas Money Launderer

A NOVEL BY T.J. Breeden

The Lion's Den

Chronicles of a Las Vegas Money Launderer

THE LION'S DEN | CHRONICLES OF A LAS VEGAS MONEY LAUNDERER. A NOVEL BY T.J. BREEDEN. IN ASSOCIATION WITH THE lbL MEDIA
GROUP. STARRING ALEX "ACE" PRYCE, JOEY SYKES, KYLE STONE, JEREMY "TRIPP" STARR, "READY," AND ANTHONY MORAINO

lbL Media Group

In association with The I*b*L Media Group.
Visit www.IbLmedia.com for more information.

ISBN: 1-44-045732-8
EAN-13: 978-14-4045732-6

This book contains suggestive content, moderate depictions of illegal acts,
& some adult language. Reader discretion is advised.

The Following is the Official Re-Release Version // "Author's Cut"

For my friend, whose strength taught me the meaning of "Survivor!"

,,,,,,,,,,,

Focus, productivity, desire, ambition, perseverance, sacrifice, & prayer –
Publication of this manuscript is proof that with hard work, <u>anything</u> is
possible… Never give up on your dreams!

Acknowledgments

. . . .

First, I thank God for the journey, and for permitting me this opportunity to artistically showcase what is becoming an increasingly obsessive love & passion for literature.

To my parents: the Reverend and First Lady of my inner sanctuary, Theodore & Mattie Breeden. You were there when I experienced some of my darkest moments; when I stopped believing & could no longer see the way. You have reinforced my faith, and continue to encourage me through moments of temporary defeat & writers block. You never gave up on me! If it weren't for you, this project would have never been possible. I love you for everything that you are, and I dedicate my life to making you proud.

To my sisters, whose support of my first project motivated me to pursue a growing enthusiasm for writing, I thank you. To my extended family, my niece & nephews, friends, and loved ones who kept pushing me to write at this level; I appreciate all of your support.

To the Emerald City of Las Vegas, Nevada for planting the seed; and to the lyrical genius of Jay-Z's "Reasonable Doubt," and "American Gangster" albums; both of which served as a stirring soundtrack to this artistic journey. Lastly, I would like to express thanks to my best friends who were nice enough to lend their personalities for character profiles.

"Thank you!"

Author's Notes

Reader Annotations & Acknowledgments:

The Lion's Den is an original story concept developed by the author and is a work of fiction. Any resemblance to actual proceedings, events, or persons, whether living or dead, is unintentional and thus coincidental.

The Connection:

"One evening, I was driving home from work and I got a phone call from an old college friend. He was in town for the evening and wanted to get a drink at a restaurant uptown, just to catch up and shoot the breeze. I was dead tired after a long day in the office, but because we go back to freshman year, I agreed. I remember walking into the bar; neck tie loose, French Cuffs rolled to my elbows, conservative sun glasses; looking like I just stepped off of the Manhattan subway, though I was some 600 miles from it. My friend was late as usual. I remember sitting down at the bar next to a local kid; throwback jersey, flashy watch; the exact opposite of my 9-5 uniform. By way of ESPN, we managed to pick-up bar chatter; first about the Maxim list, then the tone eventually switched to politics, business, and the Forbes top 100. At the time, I was considering leaving the financial services firm I was employed with and going independent. I spent most of my evenings tapping Alumni associations to grow my client list & crossover assets. Through conversation I learned that this young man was a former drug dealer who, before he had been convicted on possession charges, managed a major narcotics distribution channel, collecting high six-figure stipends in exchange for trafficking routes. He was reformed by the system & had gone legit, exchanging the street corner for a corner office. But it was interesting how although we had taken different roads in terms of occupational function, how our career paths somewhat paralleled each other."

"That's when I realized that terminology like portfolio diversification, market tampering, asset allocation, and capital gains were not the sole property of Wall Street CFO's or my Series 7 manual. These financial principles stretch across all performance-based industries that are dependent upon a salesman's ability to identify & service the insatiable needs of his client base. And though I absolutely do not condone or support the illegality of his former lifestyle, it was amazing how in terms of goal orientations, economics, financial motivations, etc., there seemed to be indirect connections between the two industries. Don't get me wrong, investment banking is a very different fundamental practice. But, what I'm trying to say is with regards to the professional & personal characteristics of CEOs who successfully manipulate the financial marketplace, and the "Cocaine Cowboys" who dominated the NBC News wires in 1980's South Beach, there are surprising likenesses."

"Here was an individual whose natural ability would've probably pushed him through brokerage licensing exams or MBA programs with ease. But he bypassed the GMAT for back alley math; and so, here we were. I was surprised at how condescending he was! When we briefly discussed the fluctuating equity markets and the then 'approaching' recession, he just blew me off! I found myself having to defend my securities license training, surprised at how well versed he was from a numbers standpoint, considering he admitted his financial education was limited to CNBC, the Wall Street Journal, and Bloomberg Reports. What separated us was simply our approach. I worked to support the greater good, freeing people of financial dependencies, while introducing rational economics and responsible financial management. But if I were hungry for commission checks, the new Benz coupe, an uptown condo, 1st class vacations, diamonds, etc., it would simply be an account dump or loaded commission sale away. Success on the streets were aligned with his ability to feed the addictions of his client book, similar to brokers who feed hope of unrealistic rates-of-return and financial guarantees. And so, greed fuels unsuitable stocks buys & investment proposals, even when their clients' risk tolerances don't suggest it. Or they churn accounts with reckless selling activity. And then there are those brokers who illegally pool cash & promise to have their clients' homes paid off in 6 months! The addiction is "Financial Freedom," the drugs are stocks that fluctuate unpredictably… I guess that's why the bottom-line refers to the operation as Broker *Dealer*."

"As he made his exit, I felt something change in my overall assessment of the industry. No, it did not affect my moral standing because I am secure in my servicing purpose. For me, it wasn't "completely" about the money. I got pleasure out of helping clients save for retirement, or to hear that my investment strategy positioned earnings to put a client's child through undergrad. At the same time, it became clearer as to how easy it is for people to be taken advantage of by crooked dealers, or perhaps, how easy it *would* be for an educated and experienced advisor to expand his client list into the illegal sectors. This kid got caught because he put his money into tangible assets as opposed to NASDAQ; because illegal pharmacists don't have bankers with sophisticated investment propositions. A double-shot of Patron introduced curiosity that would spawn this script; the story of an educated hustler with connections & interests on both sides of the track. The Lion's Den is his journey to align them."

"Real-Fiction":

"In creating this story, my goal was to draw upon the complexities & similarities shared between those who pursue a life of domestic illegality; and their white-collar counterparts whose Fortune 500 credibility is a cover for insider trading. Many of the nation's most well known purveyors of illegal activity were once corporate heads of state, whose ambitions for social elitism and luxury vacations overpowered their capacity to reason. Then there are those whose battle with the destructive ills of our inner-city communities finds them propelled into a life of crime. These are the "would've been/could've been" CEO's turned street pharmacists whose mismanaged potential eventually land them behind bars, or worse. Then, there are those who represent both. This story searches into the mindset of the hustler with youthful ambitions, Harvard credentials, limitless credibility, numerous professional designations... but instead of taking Wall Street by storm, he elects to head the most powerful and dangerous money laundering syndicate ever assembled."

"I call it "Real-Fiction." It's a story that is so fundamentally pragmatic, that it's first few chapters could easily be misinterpreted as a Forbes personal biography. My hope is that this story connects to the individual reader's sense of realism in such a way, that he/she finds it easy & perhaps enticing to overlook the fact that it's fiction, inserting themselves into the storyline and thus narrating the main character's personal journey from his/her own eyes. And though you may not agree with the characters' reasoning, my hope is that you will confer with their emotional sensibilities. The disparities of wealth in America, poverty in the inner city, pressure to conform into corporate America, the thin line between white-collar crime & legitimate promotions, lust for power & wealth, and most importantly the constant inner struggle of right & wrong. Drawing from the lead character's conflicted personality while inviting the reader to examine the contradictions that make him sincere in his pursuits, I'm hoping will give way to an entertaining & emotionally-charged artistic experience."

Style + Music = Fuel!:

"I would describe my writing style as "poetic." Though this manuscript wasn't written within the structure of the Iambic Pentameter, the use of analogies and synonyms makes this reading experience unlike any other. This project is different, not only because of its literary arrangement, but because the story's main character narrates the journey in a very honest, sophisticated, and almost lyrical tone. It is the story of Alex Pryce, an urban Ivy Leaguer who is both the product of Chicago's financial district and the inner city borough; who forwent professional designations & Wall Street Hedge Funds, for an underground cash pool & the Las Vegas strip. This storyline is poetry converged into American realism; fiction mixed with Hip-Hop's true essence of story telling. Sure, its fiction… but it is also rooted in something that is very real!"

"The Lion's Den was written beneath a soundtrack of my favorite musical artists. At times, the creative tone of this manuscript seemed to be synchronized artistically with a playlist of Hip-Hop, Alternative, Instrumentals, Gospel, Jazz, etc. Music has been the fuel to this journey, and thus has tremendously influenced my writing style. There were periods throughout the development of this project when I would literally close my eyes and type to bass & treble. Momentum built from tempo, intertwined with the emotional sequences of the storyline, made this writing process particularly smooth. And as silly as it may sound, I occasionally would act out the life of the lead character, to connect more closely with his fictional condition. I remember one Friday night in particular… I'd been working on the introductory sections for hours and decided to take a little field trip. I took an hour or so break from writing inside of a city lounge. After scoping the scene, I eventually retreated into the luxury section and just watched; envisioning the main character in his Vegas setting with Hip-Hop blasting through leather VIP booths, and credit card tabs being inflated with bottles of champagne. Once I captured the desired effect, I raced home and spent the rest of the morning staring through dark shades into Microsoft Word. To me, it was part of the process! In order for me to truly connect with the character, I sometimes needed to taste a bit of his lifestyle."

"Throughout the story, you'll notice insertions of song titles and even occasional references to specific lyrics. This is done not in an effort to reproduce the musician's work, but to credit & pay respect to how they have inspired *"my"* work. In that same tradition, I hope that this book inspires others to creatively manifest their talents and gifts artistically. It's like background music foreshadowing a theatrical climax. The songs & lyrics referenced complement the character's journey deep into… <u>The Lion's Den.</u>"

Contents

Intro: "I'm in my Zone."//

• • • • • • • • • •

"Hoover Dam... at sunset it is one of Nevada's most architecturally satisfying sites. Adjacent to an electric wasteland, surrounded by miles of empty desert air, charted in the middle of open road & approaching darkness. It's my Friday ritual. Here, I rest just beyond the wall's concrete rim some 30 minutes south east of Paris, Italy, and the Egyptian skylight. It's ironic how this stone barrier becomes my refuge every 5th workday; when the week caps and out-of-towner's check-in; while measures of impudence for the former Secretary of Commerce is demonstrated in my daily activities. Ironic, though no disrespect is intended, but it is just that: both 'Commerce' and 'Dead Presidents' which I specialize in "Secretarial" duties. In a city that moves more digits on fight night than some foreign exchanges do in an appreciated week, the dawn finds me dormant under the steering wheel, leather reclined, surrounded by dry air, lightening, and flashing bulbs in the far western distance."

Like explorers centuries before, the Chicago wind blew me westward to stake my claim in sand and precious metals. Not to be outdone, I managed to flood the boulevard with foreign currencies and pirated cash, all in the pursuit of happiness, wealth, promise... and the David Yurman black diamond collection. Like clockwork, a solace moment is interrupted by the sudden resurrection of roaring V-12's. Shades reflect, vodka influenced hands fumble over the navigation system, and the automobile's entertainment console comes alive with satellite broadcasting. A playlist intercedes, commenced by Jay-Z's "American Dreamin,'" which introduces an even deeper paradox as Hoover Dam veers left in my rear view mirror. My work itself can be characterized as a clever mix of Hip-Hop and Soul: an aggressive and sometimes contradictory performance, accentuated by passionate connection with an audience who can relate to, and thus appreciates, the story line. Just as Marvin Gaye commands the song's chorus, I am launched back into my destiny: the dreamscape that is South Las Vegas Blvd.

"I'm in my zone!" The Vegas strip reintroduces me to the at-all-cost lifestyle I've acceded to, and thus forcefully positioned myself to accept. My journey is accompanied by an Aston Martin DBS (paid for with chips from the Bellagio… true story), Cartier lenses, Armani 2-button, Oyster Perpetual time piece, and Goyard trunk luggage that doubles as an exit strategy to eventual inevitability. My life's soundtrack blasts through desert air, drowning out the constant flicker of disposable camera flashes, immigrant-pitched escort flyers, and 4-inch heels clacking dry ash fault. Eyes wonder as I speed through yet another red light, with conflicting intentions on a boulevard saturated with temptation and weekends we simply forget. The only constant is the blazing heat, which acts almost as an aphrodisiac to day-trippers looking to escape normalcy. But, with all of its voids, potholes, and redeye flights, Las Vegas is my home; and this lifestyle is and has always been my addiction.

"Friday: my favorite day of the week…"

Flash-Forward: "Speeding!" //

. . . .

"Valet!!"

You should see some of the looks I get when I drive-up in this car! The casino standards reflect through desert heat & off of the front hood like the auto paint is Colorless VS1. Tip, enter, and scope the casino floor, connecting eyes with pit bosses and of course the model bar service. Just eyes; no one gestures in this city because there are too many cameras. I visit quickly with the private high rollers' tables. This weekend draws the company of a former Senator and soon to be appointed Supreme Court Justice. He's traveling alone, so I remind the concierge to make sure that he steers free of local paparazzi. I refuel on a medium, Omaha grass-fed steak & a bottle of aged Chateau Petrus in the hotel restaurant. I'll admit that I'm an animal of habit, having preserved the same Friday evening reservation for the past several months. But this evening; it's as if my senses have been heightened and everything looks clearer, tastes cleaner, and feels cooler. This is an important weekend; both for me, and for my organization. Hundreds of millions of dollars migrate to a city blanket with sand, intolerable temperatures, and the awe inspiring water fountain from "Ocean's 11" to place their wagers on even dryer hopes & the proclaimed future of sport. The Merlot tastes sweeter this evening, because hundreds of millions of dollars will also be shifted from my portfolio books to casino vaults for deposit, wagering, leverage... but more importantly to be cleaned.

Amidst foreshadowing of a Main Event that will change the face of Las Vegas' financial imprint (as well as legitimize my professional influence), the transformation from private banker to playboy activates as I close out my dinner tab. Tonight, I'll celebrate what will be the "put your money up" moment that my Columbia University education assured me, which now seems many, many loan payments ago. Imagine the sovereignty of knowing your influence reaches everything with an 'S.' on its Las Vegas Blvd address. Now, imagine the struggle of assuming guilty knowledge associated with laundering criminal numbers beneath the watchful eye of every floor camera on the strip. I exit back into the Vegas night, speeding through red lights just as I had on approach from Hoover Dam. But again my "zone" imposes itself through the gas pedal like an alter ego or a dissociative identity hungry for the destruction of its host.

510hp pilots me South on the boulevard to what I like to call 'Freedom.' The lobby is flooded with dreamers pretending to be what ironically I've convinced the FBI that I am not! It's funny how mall security guards become fighter pilots and gym-rats become professional wrestlers when they touch down at McCarran International. 'Freedom,' with its electric backdrop and dynamic viewpoint, elevates me above the strip like a throne to survey all at which I've manipulated numerically. Well, perhaps soapbox is a better way to describe my platform, considering the source of my revenue stream is laundered cash. It is a natural habitat for TMZ celebutantes who suggest that they desire to stay unseen in the VIP, yet continuously requests that the DJ announce "[blank] is in the F'n building!!" My crew is already here: Stone, Tripp, 'Ready,' and Sykes; my boys from college who became virtual shareholders & partners in my laundering operation. Together we've financially infiltrated what the Nevada Gaming Commission has considered impenetrable, and successfully do what the SEC and Supreme Court would consider 30 to Life!

Again I'm a creature of habit, so as I survey the night from the same corner, crimson, booth I'm careful to stay below radar and off camera phones. Everywhere you look you see potential DWIs fueled by cleavage and open bar tabs that are constantly being inflated amidst the shuffle. You can always tell who's visiting Vegas for the first time. It's usually marked by too much alcohol, vomit, broken heels, random aggressiveness, C-Notes spilled over club balconies, and of course an obnoxious need to feel special. It's like an Ant Farm; same sand, same disorderly movement, same capacity filled glass space; only with liquid hallucinogen and a velvet rope. And although I haven't checked bags, taken bets, or upgraded suites, there's no denying that I'm somewhat responsible for the weekend vibe that attracts 5 hour flights from the East coast. Who'd look at a young, black man in a European inspired sports car and assume anything other than the 3rd year reserve for the Utah Jazz or maybe the Broncos Strong Safety? It's because of a skill I picked up years ago that tomorrow, casino cash-cages maintain $400 million dollar holding levels in preparation for lucky first time winners, and 40-1 underdogs like "Buster" Douglas.

"Introduce Vodka!"

I'll admit, since moving out west I've become ever the social opportunist, contrary to the shell I inhabited as an undergrad in the Big Apple. I could spit digits with the best of them during market hours, and eventually evolved to charm my way through happy hour. I credit my uptown experiences for nerves that seem to instinctively tab bottles of over-priced Armand de Brignac in response to a welcoming gaze from an adjacent booth.
"Barman, a bottle for those ladies as well... Also, could you deliver that calla lily arrangement that they make in the hotel restaurant? Of course I'll pay extra!!"
Ever the hopeless romantic... These moments seem to have a way of forcing me to rewind, where I help myself to memories of poetically inspired love letters, 'slow jam mix-tapes,' and of course: "No, I love *you* more!!" Those same nerves seem to have been replaced with bond certificates, insider information, and: "No, put it on *my* tab!!" It's funny how a change of environment can change your mind.

Champagne via 'special delivery' happens just about everyday in Vegas. Lucky me I guess, that I've been able to enjoy the type of cash flowing lifestyle that treats VIP like drop-change for the Salvation Army bucket. Bar servers keeps bottles of Rosé on constant approach like Boeings at the McCarran tarmac. And as I peered through the crowded dance floor to ensure delivery, we connect eyes. She glares down to a trimmed, lily arrangement floating in the ice bucket, then back to me. The moment introduces a chill into my comfort zone that's inconsistent with the person I've become beyond velvet ropes. Business partners, pit bosses, none of which intimidate me the slightest. But this woman's stare reinforces regret in my daily conduct, making me wish I were just a hotel concierge with 700 square feet on the North Strip and not, well… me!

Though I hardly chase the boulevard, I do seem to live out a sort of subconscious social strategy. Let's face it; I wash money for criminal syndicates, disguising illegal activity as legitimate returns. And although I've chosen this conflicted lifestyle, I'm still very much my mother's son and a gentleman like my father. I'm as much an admirer of jazz & oil paintings, as I am of international currencies & hedge funds. Everything about Las Vegas is polarizing. So, considering my 9-5 consists of managing offshore financials, I find balance in the form of sexy Peace Corp volunteers and madam CEOs with 501(c)(3) paperwork. Besides, I can't assume every beautiful woman in Vegas is just trying to pass beyond velvet ropes or passenger the Aston… right?

Suddenly, her silhouette fills my view; bringing her within reach of my reality.
Hi, uhm…"
She sits. With her left hand, she removes my shades and folds them neatly into my inner jacket pocket. As my eyes struggle to become adjusted to the streaming lights, she leans in over my right shoulder and speaks to me. "When I was a little girl, my father would pick calla lilies and roses for me and my mother every Friday on his way home from work… it was sort of a weekend ritual that goes back to how they first met." I was in disbelief! It wasn't as if counter intel & background information were being fed to me through a hidden earpiece. "…Unfortunately, I lost him a few years ago. I thought I'd never receive something like this again. And here in this dark, Vegas nightclub, there it was… stemless; resting inside of my champagne flute."

The music dies as she looks deep into my expression, seemingly in search of a response other than "it was a coincidence." I'm speechless, unknowing of whether she's angry for being reminded of a hurtful memory, or at peace by the apparent twist of fate. She leans in closer, placing the flower buds to my cheek and speaking so close into my ear that I can feel her voice run down my spine.

"Who are you?" She giggles, and with a deep exhale I can almost feel her body settle next to me. "I need to know… I'm willing to disregard the game, the Vegas setting, and even the circumstances at which I'm meeting you." She breaks into the warmest smile I've seen in years, something reminiscent of Christmas morning. "I don't usually respond to these types of things, but there's something here, right here in your eyes… I'll sit here all night if it takes that long. This small gesture reaches deep inside of who I am, and… I need to know… I need to know who *you* are."

Moments later my eyes adjust to the lights, and yes; she does look familiar. A likeness of her body wraps a La Perla billboard on the most southern end of the strip. Her eyes would lead me back into Sin City from excursions at Hoover Dam… those same eyes seem to offer me salvation now.

"My name's Vicky…"

Every time she moves it's almost as if the lights adjust accordingly. We sit for a while, and she tells me about her life, what she likes, and where she's been. We dance, and she grinds into my body so closely that under stage lighting, our complexions intertwine.

"Barman, I'm covering that table for the rest of the night… put it on my tab, whatever they want, ok?" I had to; I didn't want any bored or thirsty girlfriends interrupting what had become the most welcoming connection I'd generated since I arrived on the strip years prior.

Minutes turn to hours, and a night's bar tab turns into rent money. Victoria rests her chin on my shoulder, playfully jerking my ear closer to her. "What do you think of us going someplace so we can be alone, perhaps where we don't have to wait for table service, and it's a little less crowded?" She places her hand on my chest, and then to the inner pocket she'd visited earlier to remove my sunglasses. "I'm here through Thursday for a calendar shoot, and I can just… you know… catch up with my girls tomorrow… That's unless you still have other bottles and 'coincidences' to pay out before you close your tab!"

Seduction stares deep into my vodka affected consciousness. Club bass and glaring effects tear through the dark booth like lightening in the empty desert sky. It's been a long time since I've met someone who makes me laugh this much. She makes it easy for me to just be myself, inviting me to put aside the Vegas caricature and enjoy the moment. In the midst of what seems so innocent, the short drive north on the boulevard has me questioning my own sincerities. Is this another random hook-up, or perhaps an unearthed subconscious infatuation from months of admiring her face aside a lonely desert highway? Is it natural chemistry, the rarity of the moment, or the several top floor penthouse suites I rent across the strip that seems to have her jaded? The Palazzo, Caesars, the Bellagio… I asked her which *suite* she was "in the mood for" like we were ordering dessert take-out. But in a way, I guess she sort of is dessert… something *sweet* I was in the mood for.

3:00a.m. and the MGM is packed! Again, walking through a casino lobby, this time attempting to avoid looks from those who would recognize Vicky from the south strip ad. The elevator doors close around her body, and my sexual rise is almost synchronized with the floor gauge. Even if I weren't influenced by intoxication, I still could've peaked at the sheer site of her. A key unlocks access to the top floor, where the Vegas strip electrifies the skylight, and at dawn the distant mountains resemble a dry haze of cigar smoke. It was almost as if she'd stepped down from a billboard to accompany me into the perfect fantasy; her frame wrapped in the same La Perla piece from the ad. We laugh, toast, tease, pull, and twist; sharing love in a fixed madness of two people that are seemingly conjoined at the pelvis. We share a sexual desire that resembles something almost cerebral, and ironically both have a tendency to smile uncontrollably after we've 'arrived!' And even as the moment concludes amidst bubble bath and brief pillow talk, nothing has changed. When the dawn settles, my lifestyle will only accommodate one, washing away her perfume like the cash I launder for a living.

The alarm clock wakes me to find Victoria's smile, dressed only in calla lily buds, my sun lenses no less, and the desert sun peaking through hotel blinds. There's room service and a phone number on the coffee table. "I hope you like 'em scrambled. I'll give these shades back tonight… ringside, right?!" I have to admit, I kinda' dig that! I consider tossing the note to the trash but who am I kidding. We had a great time and besides, a girl like her stays picture ready!! A smirk leads dry eyes back on into to the dawn in preparation for the mega event of the summer! Today will be my inauguration, dedicated to years of being disregarded as a talented upstart in Chicago's financial district. Dedicated to the chop-shop where I honed the very skill that propelled me into the inner circles that run this town. Dedicated to consortiums of influential men who shook Joe Louis' hand on this same Las Vegas Blvd, 40 years prior to my arrival.

Today, "I'm in my zone!!"

"Valet!!"

Salutation: "I am..."//

••••••••••

"I live in the land of kings, where Sinatra entertained the likes of JFK years before the UFC invaded the strip. Amidst shadows cast by glass high risers in the one US city that exists to see the underdog triumph, I've catapulted an underground syndicate into one of the most powerful illegal financiers in the country. My presence alone threatens to clear more checks & longstanding records than Lebron; and like him, casino owners benefit from my skill like David Stern, the Nike machine, and the rest of the Jordan re-branding crew. I'm at war with floor managers who scour down from the casino eye, and drug infested streets that capture & destroy young wombs. I'm the unknown force that sustains this city's economic pulse. I re-up center floor blackjack at the MGM Grand, Woolite cash for some of the biggest illegal corporations in the world, conclude each night on my knees in prayer, and start every morning with $100 on black. I've seen fights fixed and yes, I know what's behind the curtain of Cirque du Soleil. Let's just say, I start where you finish!"

L as Vegas is congested with "wonderers;" the dreamers with financial ambitions to corner the illegal markets and flood small-time bookies with big-dollar wagers. On their best day, these kids couldn't table my worst account. I often refer to them simply as "Fan Man." Remember Bowe vs. Holyfield II? It's a synonym for an uncalculated & misdirected collapse from the apex of "my kinda" success! They have no respect for the craft. Instead they presume that they can simply wire a few hundred thousand here or there without the district attorney's office noticing their ridiculous spending habits. The operation is similar to chess: strategizing 2 moves from the next. Or blackjack: calculating the percentages and knowing when to double-down. In a city where casino bulbs seem to fade a little everyday, & then recover with each sell-out, De la Hoya comeback, or multi-million dollar cage deposit, "tomorrow" is a strategic anomaly. I take in the warmth of the desert sunset and I find peace at a bridge whose namesake conflicts with the very fiber at which I generate my lifestyle. Resting aside Hoover every Friday at day's end, yet I'm able to evade and wash my hands of the Federal Bureau with each bill laundered. "I'm in my zone" so deep that the streets appear translucent under SLR head lamps and behind Montblanc lenses. They all want me to fall; or behind bars; or hung by my ankles beneath the "Welcome" sign to warn off enthusiast with ambitions to reshuffle the deck.

"But they can't deny me!" I run the most powerful illegal financing operations in the US. The boulevard is the jungle, temptation is the Beast, and sin is King! Some call me a handicapper; a drip-man, substitution banker, but my clients and the kids down at the group home simply call me "Ace." The MGM Grand logo solidified my hustle, and now stands as a monument to my royalty.

"My name is Alex Pryce… Welcome to the Lion's Den."

Level One: Background Check

••••••••••

"I was groomed a believer... but I was built to be a money launderer."

Chapter 1: Interrogation //

"I'm out for Dead Presidents to represent me!"

My life has been dedicated to the fulfillment of this simple pursuit. From the beginning of my career on the Chicago Exchange floor, or even perhaps earlier when I worked odd jobs to afford my Columbia certificate, I was thirsty for big commission checks, huge cash purchases, island vacations with no luggage, and private jets to... wherever! It's the lifestyle exhibited from which this very lyric was quoted. The life that MTV flaunts, what VH1 documents, even Forbes releases lists annually to see who's new & which names have been shuffled to the top. CNBC reports it daily from 9:30am to the 4 o'clock closing bell. Athletes dispute contracts and "hold out" for the rights to negotiate higher levels of it, and even politicians have huge benefit dinners to raise it. The world revolves around which country has less of it in their respective national deficits, and the US fights to maintain its global relevance in terms of maintaining international ascendancy, hoping that the value of "ours" flourishes while our allies' diminishes. "Dead Presidents!"

You hear about CEO's on television that are forced out of their jobs, yet safely transition into the private sector with platinum parachutes in excess to $50 million dollars. How hedge fund managers earn 8-figure salaries for betting opposite the market bubble. This subsequently makes me think about a friend who plays the lottery every week, hoping that a scratch-off card will deliver free earnings to hedge against a salary that's not covering rising costs of gas, groceries, and healthcare. The balance of freedom and power is leveraged for those who acquire, multiply, save, and hand down wealth to future generations. The American Dream fulfilled!

"I never had that…"

I never experienced the reassurance of knowing wealth & opportunity had already been established on my behalf, which would crutch feelings of disappointment if I didn't get into the college of my choosing, if I didn't get the job, or if that business I tried to start just never caught fire. Like most, I was forced to accept the deck's inconsistencies and hope that the dealer busts! However, unlike most I'd turn an entry level job into a six figure cash pool, dominating an untargeted market that generates hundreds of millions of dollars per month. It is the sector of illegal activity that stays constant regardless of inflation. I pushed the limits of the Broker Dealer rule book and the SEC regulations binder, until it made room for me to push an AMG through stiff, uptown Chicago traffic. It was hunger and ambition that fueled my contempt for a social practice that sets aside opportunity and allocated funds for those that never even asked for it. Like those sons of connected bureaucrats who got stoned before semester finals and were handed the exam as a prep tool, while I crammed through dry, sleep deprived vision; jacked on "NoDoz" and Rap music.

My story begins with these alliances, partnerships, and corporate biases that separate the hustlers from the privileged. I rarely express my disgust for those who had it and never earned it. Even as I extended myself through overtime and extra credit, I always seemed fingertips away from the top shelf. I'd work so hard just to excel through limited expectations, in a game that had been fixed in favor of the connected. Who's blaming the system? I'm just stating what has become an obvious truth. From the steps of Columbia University, I watched stock brokers scramble to Wall Street, searching for the next big score. Some would visit the B-School and speak about the pride they feel walking into their office every morning. They'd gloat how their roots could be traced generations to men who traded OTC (over-the-counter), establishing their mark on the Exchange before there was NASDAQ. They bragged about how they were appointed the youngest partner in the firm, vacation in the Caymans, and married the Vicky Secrets model on the Times Square billboard. In this industry, the hierarchy and value of one's network ultimately determines the types of groceries that were brought home. I made up my mind long ago that I wasn't going to be the guy drowning in debt & shots of cheep vodka while "the youngest partner in the firm" sun bathed on the top deck of his family's yacht. I'd reach the top shelf… even at the expense of the ethics code.

Cornering the markets, price manipulation, product displacement; all were tactics I was familiar with growing up on the South Side of Chicago. I'd later find that these methods were as common in white collar corruption as they were in pushing street medicine. Though I never sold drugs, I always had a fascination with the hustle. And as I got older I noticed strange parallels between my job, and what the neighborhood boys did. The chase for the big score, getting clients hooked on the taste; the only difference is the Dow Jones is legal; and unlike the corner, the internet made access to my products limitless. It was a hustle that didn't service the disconnected dreamer who wanted to make a difference, just the network feasting entrepreneur who wanted to make fast money. Two lines of business… disconnected but congruent; opposite but parallel. But, what if one could submerge these worlds together? Who would exercise such an unwise philosophy, or perhaps who would be gifted enough to corner, manipulate, and displace an untapped economic waterfall? What if someone who had an understanding & even a respect for the street, could knot that with an Ivy League education and a disassociated outlook of how wealth is unfairly distributed in-house? What if the scales were adjusted and I benefited from the same system of elitism I condemned? What if? I asked myself these questions constantly during my college days in upper Manhattan. Today I've answered them, and consequently have also been forced into more strenuous lines of questioning, usually under duress and police interrogation.

"*Who the hell do you think you are?*"

That's usually how it begins. I hear this kind of BS all of the time. Sure, I'm pushing 30, but I'm still the youngest to retain reserved ringside seating at MGM Grand. The casino pit bosses love my skill for identifying foreign currency to swell their weekend cage deposits. The promoters love the big ticket gamblers who drive the odds up to levels that tempt them to wage against their own fighters! The Gaming Commission wants to question me, and the FBI wants me to snitch. Though reluctantly unashamed, I've decided to forgo legitimate IRA transfers in exchange for seven-figure cash imbursements, Euros, occasional insider information, and BlueStar connectors that depart & land On-Demand like Time Warner. I was groomed a believer… but I was built to be a money launderer.

• • • • • • • • • • • •

"Because many of the success stories chartered by Forbes were lists of entrepreneurs, White Sox, and Headliners with aspirations of going "Pro" early, just like I did. We all had that in common; whether it's on the playing field, or on white-collar Exchange corners, "Hustle" is what clears big checks!"

Chapter 2: Uptown Tryouts //

"I was expected to achieve great things in the name generational success."

Burdened with this idealism of a natural ability which I was heir to inherit, from great men in my adopted family whose last name and recognized accomplishments were well documented (at least they were locally). We never had the connections that others had, I never made the grades in college that others did. But I honed skills that professors didn't tutor. A proficiency that accreditation committees and writers of the academic calendar refused to make a college pre-requisite… Hustle! It was what accelerated people like me ahead of the success curve, and also kept us below the radar gun. I had a way with people, and natural instincts that made up for theoretical deficiencies; such as a short attention span that forced my own personal interests into submission, in an effort to take what my Sociology Professor was saying seriously.

Think of it like a star college athlete with ambitions of going pro early. The constellations seem to align when coaches and GMs begin to actively recruit his talents. Consider the excitement one feels when he realizes that he's mentally and physically ready to make an impact at the next level. That's how I felt, ready to step out of my college dorm, and accept the immediate challenge of identifying what my life's purpose was. This simple ideal has framed my journey, and as I earned my undergraduate ticket to the corporate acceptance party, it became even more of the focal point. College ended, & life began. I was the one who was always content to exchange an MD, MBA, PhD, etc. for a go-getter's mentality, slick tongue, acceptance to risk, and an undeniable ability to identify opportunities! That's just me, no disrespect to all of my friends who are very well-off working the 9-5, driving Range Rovers with baby seats strapped to the backseat, and Hannah Montana CDs in all 6 disk slots. I was bred & groomed for the life that revolved around self-made successes and rewards that, if trailed, could come back to me with dire consequences.

Four and a half years of Columbia just to ignore the entire commencement ceremony. To me, the B.S. I earned was just that, BS! Don't get me wrong, the certificate offers me access to relationships and resources I otherwise would not have been able to tap. And of course, college girls are worth 4+ years of exams! But I couldn't shake this feeling that when it came down to examining what would make me successful, it would be a raw capacity to gravitate toward opportunities, and the courage to accept the challenge; none of which are pre-requisites of academia. It's just not for all of us. In the career life that would place me inside Italian leather seats, and would eventually dim my view via Cartier lenses, what I had was enough... Hustle! I remember sitting across the desk from the Sr. Partner of a prominent firm in uptown Chicago who asked me "What would your friends say is your number one attribute?" My mind quickly went to a rehearsed answer: "He works hard, is a team player, and has natural leadership qualities..." etc. But my mouth opened and uttered a very honest and seemingly untamed response. I very reluctantly said "He hustles!!" As awkward as that moment was, I was offered the job that very same evening! Because many of the success stories chartered by Forbes were lists of entrepreneurs, White Sox, and Headliners with aspirations of going "Pro" early, just like I did. We all had that in common; whether it's on the playing field, or on white-collar Exchange corners, "Hustle" is what clears big checks. My grasp of this made me a top prospect. Most went on to teach, or stay in pursuit of a Masters to defer those student loans just a little longer. So while others were turning graduate level tassels and listening to how great the other side of commencement was, I was touring the Chicago Mercantile Exchange and preparing to embrace the inevitable journey towards my own 'Pro Draft.' Guess that made me a Top Pick!

Contrary to my humble beginnings, I quickly developed a thirst for champagne, congratulatory speeches, flashbulbs, & courtside seats. I wanted more than the normal life I was heir to inherit from foster-parents who, though honorably, accepted stewardship in exchange for investment holdings. I watched them strain endlessly to provide for me on teacher's salaries that never seemed to support our needs. They dedicated their lives to grooming the potential of students whom they influenced. With all due respect to those responsible for getting me here, that was not the life that I wanted. My parents, both educators, I think were just happy to see me "graduate" into a state of mind that would reject misdemeanors and the temptation of illegal trafficking that wrecked the lives of the neighborhood boys I ran with. College was an escape from an inevitable life on the South Side streets that had captured all of my high school friends like bear traps.

That paper certificate was more for their gratification and acceptance than it was to legitimize my own purpose. Imagine me a teacher; what in the world would I teach? I could have probably chalk boarded a curriculum that would simply be a truth-telling session, but from my perspective it might have been little biased. I was encouraged to follow my dreams and aspirations, reaching far beyond street corners, drug infested high-rises, alcohol soaked gutters and illegal usage of the 2nd amendment. What university accreditation committee would approve a course that promotes this level of free & open thinking? Besides, you can't teach someone how to hustle. Entrepreneurs are bred in response to a specific need. For most it's to make money, for some it's to make a different, for others it's freedom. For me, it was about the money… period! From as far back as sophomore year, my focus was to earn enough notes to live my life courtside to the same pro's I constantly compare my journey with. I used college as the means to build my network. Literally, ever week there was a CEO on campus visiting a colleague in the business school, or a Sr. Vice President sitting in the stands watching Conference or Inter-League play.

I remember my first job on campus, contacting alumni and requesting contributions for a new med lab or athletic facility. These were people who made millions of dollars a year doing… something. Seemingly every week one of these phone calls would lead to a discussion of how he or she "graduated with a degree in Art History, and ended up making millions from the internet bubble." There was one conversation I remember vividly with an alumni who apologized for returning my call several days late, but he had been vacationing in the south of France (spur of the moment kind of thing), celebrating millions made in venture capital deals and an explosion on the stock market. This kind of stuff happens everyday; success stories that are basically happenstance and perfect timing. Of course, these individuals valued their time in school. But it was real life experience, a little luck, and a willingness to take risks to which they accredit their success. See the wheels turning? So, I began training for tryouts.

My skill-set was ideal to work the Chicago stock markets. I was young, fearless, unafraid of rejection, eager to learn, motivated by money, and was familiar with the marketplace seeing as how I was born and raised in the city. I was able to tap into networks that hadn't yet been infiltrated, i.e. the South Side. Though gentrification in certain urban areas was on the rise, there were other developing districts that were experiencing growth from within, and thus uptown was competing to put cash into the boroughs in the interest of maintaining what was then considered "social integrity." Basically, the community was investing into itself! Funny thing, the uptown firms were just as pleased to see this initiative, because each wanted to be the first to demonstrate "compassion" and "support" for the area by volunteering services. So even though the community was reinvesting, a lack of urban banks meant they were indebted to uptown for the loan money. Thus, a young, anxious, black kid walking in the door was just the promotional tool these firms needed to "make daddy feel good about his little girl dating the preppy boy across town."

I still remember my first day on the job. I wore a dark suit, white French cuff, and a silk red double Windsor. Imagine Sidney Poitier at age 22; the same debonair bearings, mixed with his Carl Lee resolve from "A Raisin in the Sun." It was like selling candy at recess. Just stay true to the price, allow value to determine demand for the product, complete the transaction, manage it, and rebalance every 3 months or so (at least, that was my understanding via CNBC & Econ 10). For the first few years, I played at the big boys table, starting my career with one of "the big 5."

You know the global market firms that literally run the US financial districts? 7 months from my first day, I was licensed to sell anything of value on any Exchange in the US. It was an irresistible power surge, to be just beyond drinking age and be granted fiduciary responsibilities to millions of dollars under management. Most of my friends had never seen $100 G's in one place. One of my first transactions was a deposit of $1.5 million, just to let it sit in the money market until we determined suitable investment opportunities. I'm talking real money, the kind that makes you excited just to wire it! Even though it wasn't mine, the power I felt to make the call instructing a transfer of a half of a mill was a huge adrenalin rush!

I was introduced to true wealth. Not cash, anyone could flash a knot of hundreds. But the kind of money that pays seven figures in taxes, and changes their voter registration from blue to red, irrespective of political views, but just in principle to their ever-changing income bracket. I learned that 'real money' cuts out coupons and drives a Toyota Camry during the week, because they owned municipal bonds, had 529's for each of their grandchildren, owned a stake in the Cubs, and made smart investments that attract high returns, not high levels of attention. 'Real Money' wasn't the 4th year guard who dropped $100K on a supercharged Rover, but his boss who has the power to trade him away mid-season for something of greater potential value, like stock options or baseball cards. That's real money, real power… that's what I wanted. The kind of money that matters; not diamond time-pieces with limited battery life, but real estate that is limited to those who exceed a predetermined net worth. I found myself dreaming of a life at which no luxury would be beyond my reach, and the exclusions that barred me from enjoying the greater benefits of the America Dream would now be dismantled. But after four years of building networks and hoping to emerge from the cubical to an isle office, I was still generations away from beach front property. With all of these transfers, rollovers, huge deposits, credibility, business card bragging rights, and beautiful top floor office space that saw square to the United Center, I was still suffering from the entry-level wage that sucked my friends back into classrooms. Late hours were expected, but didn't necessarily translate into income. I soon realized that these crumbs were similar to the empty-promise filled commencements I decided to forego a few years prior.

The firms wanted someone with my mentality, my drive, my network, my hustle, even my Columbia, but they also wanted someone who wouldn't walk into the Sr. Partner's office and say "where's my cut and why is everyone else getting a bigger share?" I wasn't intimidated by marble desks or suits with higher thread counts. It was at that moment that I recognized something that would become my strongest professional asset; I realized the value my own personal worth. It's not just being confident in who you are, nor is it condescension. But it was very simply placing a dollar value after my name, the same way my comrades placed initials as symbols of accreditation and demos of achievement. A powerful discovery that upon proper manipulation, propelled my career faster than anyone perhaps in the history of this industry... that is, if I can truthfully consider myself to be part of the industry considering my exploitation of the ethics code. Perhaps it was selfish, but as I grew, I learned that it was just as important to promote myself as it was the logo on my business card. The firm's name was on the side of athletic parks and every piece of correspondence I used to market. So it was up to me to demonstrate my own worth and make the distinction between the two. Combining street smarts with what essentially is the white boy hustle made me an especially dangerous hire, and I was developing a first rate Master's education in a value added, need-based, quick handed transaction system similar to the one I'd observed for years on the South Side. This version was legitimate, in most cases. I'd soon be introduced to the latter, which now has become the basis of my Las Vegas operation.

Then, that day... it was a Friday and it felt something like the first day of spring. I was approaching the five-year mark, and feeling more and more like Carl Lee in reference to "the dream deferred." I had basically refused to be monogamist; trading and brokering for this firm then another, before I finally decided it was time to move to a place where appreciation for my skills would be demonstrated in their acknowledgement that Roman Noodles isn't dinner, and 500 square feet is no way to live! I received an invitation to interview with an unfamiliar group who based their shop out of an office park 20 miles outside of the city. This moment, this exact moment is where the streets of Chicago seemed to shift and money really began to grow in the Wrigley outfield. I look at my life now, in the desert city where cash does literally fall from oblivion, and underground vaults beneath check-in counters hold millions of dollars. My luck & success is due in part to a burning desire ignited by this six story chop-shop firm…. where I made my first million before my 28th birthday… where I legitimized hundreds of millions of illegal earnings… where I attended workouts in preparation for the Uptown Las Vegas Tryouts.

• • • • • • • • • •

"The dice are loaded kid. Be smart and cash in while it's hot!"

Chapter 3: Bleach //

"In the interest of time, I'll skip a few months… from the uptown high rise to the factory shop in a small office park, 25 miles or so north of the Jordan statue."

Here in this six-story converted warehouse, I felt valuable, was treated as a partner, and more importantly was able to determine my own financial worth. We shared a common motivation; the only things that mattered were: (1) the numbers, (2) the clients, and (3) "at the end of each month, make sure the revenue generation levels are exceeded!" No one in the building was better at covering the spread than me. I just had natural abilities that worked well with the hustle. Like for instance over previous years, I learned to memorize client info; eventually I was able to recite my entire rolodex without notes. So even while compliance officers from my previous employers watched me box my shit up, I was able to transfer most of the big accounts to the new firm. I treated it as a mental exercise. Today it proves to be invaluable skill. I didn't consider the benefit of not having names and numbers listed in my Vertue mobile until Vegas city vice confiscated it, and tried to transfer numbers out.

Within 8 months of my first day, I was managing 8-figures in assets. It was a great time in my professional history. My new commission schedule was twice that of the uptown branches, and they even moved me out of a cubical to a small hallway office with a young, attractive assistant. Now, I can't expect everyone to understand what any of this means, but for a 27 year old industry neophyte to be managing this level of currency is a big deal, especially when it guarantees enough quarterly fee-income to expand my living situation beyond 500 sq. feet. Things were great, and then… another Friday morning. A morning I wish I would've called in sick, or was on vacation, or even had a little finder-bender in the parking deck that delayed my arrival. The elevator opened and my assistant tells me that my "9 o'clock was waiting in my office." I hadn't scheduled an appointment for that morning. I almost never clocked meetings on Friday, and had planned to only be in the office for a few hours; you know, just to get an early jump on the next week. There'd never been a morning where someone was sitting and waiting for me to arrive. I'd never been late for a face-to-face and normally didn't take walk-ins. So for someone to be waiting for me was rather odd.

Waiting was an older gentleman who had to have known I was confused by his presence.
"Mr. Pryce?" he asks.
"That's me. I'm sorry; I didn't realize I had scheduled an appointment this morning."
"We aren't scheduled; you came as a referral from a colleague of mine in South Florida. My partners and I do business upstairs in the Investment Banking department. We asked for an introduction; they said that you're the best broker on the floor, and that I should bring my business to you if I want it done correctly!" I'm flattered, but let's be honest about something: nobody upstairs, or in this business for that matter, EVER passes money onto someone else unless they want something out of it, don't know what to do with it, or of course if they're scared to touch it!

He goes on "My name is Anthony Moraino. I have a few businesses on the coast and in the islands. My partners and I are transitioning ownership, and I'm looking to establish a few holding accounts to settle my involvement into cash and securities... you know, places to earn some interest while the lawyers finish the sale of my positions."
"Hmm... No Sir, I don't think I know exactly. What types of businesses are you involved in? Real Estate, Development, Entertainment..."
"Well..." he interrupts, "...it's all sorts of things, and it's a little complicated. But what I need is someone who's not intimidated by large deposits, is thorough with transaction instructions, and of course is not afraid to earn big commissions."
"Hmm..." Strange.

He's got the look of an uptown hot shot; very corporate, wool blend 2-button suit, French cuffs, silk pocket square, and Omega wrist wear. So, why is he 20 miles from the city Exchange looking to settle & invest money here? As much as I appreciate this firm's pay schedule and disliked my uptown employee experience, the city is the first place I would go if I had some loose stacks and wanted to move them.
"Well, I'm definitely not intimidated by big numbers, and my time is worth every penny." I'll admit I had gotten a little cocky; it more or less comes with the job. What can I say, I was 27, a top earner in the building, didn't particularly need his business, and was skeptical that he had anything worth my time on top of that! Having already worked high net-worth clients, I wasn't affected by expensive suits, nor did I ever feel the need to chase digits. He even smirked at my response, as if it were exactly what he wanted to hear. This was the second time I got this type of look from an "off the cuff" response, so to speak. The first time I got a job offer. So yeah; apparently I was pretty dialed-in!

"So, what exactly are you looking to do?" He reaches into the inner pocket of his sports coat and pulls out a check.
"I need to deposit this, preferably in a money market to start so I can keep it liquid, just in case I need to transfer it into another business account, set up a Trust Fund for the kids, or maybe buy a vacation home! I'm not sure exactly what I want to do yet, but I'll know as soon as the deals go through." He hands it to me and continues, "This is the first of what will be several deposits of this size or greater. I just opened a corporate account upstairs in the name of a holding company as a means of setting up the umbrella for all of my business activities. They said that I wouldn't have to complete any additional paperwork, and that it could be pulled from the system and opened internally..." I unfold the check... it's as if the room goes completely silent and dark, with a high resolution beam gleaming directly onto the check's valuation line.

A $31,439,546.21 certified check that had been 'Signature Guaranteed' by an offshore bank and confirmed by the investment banking department upstairs. I was speechless, seemingly paralyzed with disbelief. At that moment, I was reminded of expressed levels of resentment for those whom opportunities to create wealth had been gift wrapped. How some people just get the breaks that the rest of us don't, and how the Wrigley outfield turned into cash when rookies were brought up from the minor leagues. I begin calculating commissions and lose count; even temporarily lost consciousness under the influence shock & disbelief, as if they had been shaken over ice & served straight!

   "Ok." I got my head back in the game now. I place the note face-up in the center of my desk, leaning back in my office chair to create a little distance between myself and what I then associated with a very luxurious financial future! "Who upstairs did you talk to?" Silence… Anthony looks confused for several seconds, almost in awe that I was even asking questions and had returned from my noticeable temporary lapse.
"Uh, I'm not sure, some young fellow… but, he told me that you could take care of this for me. He said you were the guy to take on this type of action! "Go see Pryce!" is what he said."
Hmm… Silence again. I begin again, "Well…"
He interrupts, leans in, and stabs his index finger onto the signature line of the financial score lying on the oak desk. "Now, let me be clear… this will probably be the easiest million dollars you'll ever make son. I'm not big on details, and I don't like to explain myself or my business. I just need to make deposits, transfers, and withdrawals when necessary… I'm looking for someone who knows what others don't know and likes it that way… somebody that pays attention to details and can do without the specifics! Now, is that you, or do I need to take my business uptown? Trust me; they'll give me an assistant and a parking space for what I'm bringing!"

   It was clear to me at this point. Some numbers-crunchers and brokers get caught in money laundering jobs because they never see the signs. They deposit huge checks, believe things like "the money's for a Trust Fund," and exchange Yen for bills without a second thought. Not me, I knew exactly what this was. For this to have been such an easy hand-off, someone upstairs was being commissioned for this introduction.

Criminals are of the most paranoid species, having to always keep their heads on a swivel in efforts to stay one step ahead of 3-letter agencies. And here, sitting in my office filled with audacity, 8-digits were folded on the table like a bad Texas Hold 'em hand. Who drops $31 mill, and doesn't even care to hear the details of what happens next? It's the type of person who offers camaraderie & sneaker money to the corner boys in exchange for loyalty. Only difference is, neighborhood hustlers didn't have the weight or the balls to walk into my office or any like it, and drop a White Sox signing bonus in the desk. Yeah, I knew what this was, just so there's no confusion. Considering my current, it should be pretty obvious what my response was.

      I remember walking Anthony Moraino to the elevator. He told me that he'd connect with me in a few days with transaction instructions after he talks to his partners in Miami. We shook hands, then that all too familiar smirk crept across his chin as he seemed to fade into the back of the elevator.

"Lear Jets, Italian sports cars, Euros, private beaches, foreign exchanges, tailor made suits, and ringside seats… The dice are loaded kid. Be smart and cash in while it's hot!" The doors slide closed and I'm left holding what could basically be considered a bank issued lottery ticket. I just stood there, staring at my reflection in the elevator steel hoping that it would offer something other than more questions. Anthony Moraino… He never signed a single line of paperwork, nor did he provide a shred of physical identification. Anthony Moraino, who came into my office as a referral from an unknown investment banker upstairs and walked in with a $31 million dollar cash order. In accepting the deposit (or by simply holding the note in my hand), I was violating every federal banking and securities regulation in the book. And although it temporarily ate away at my conscious, I couldn't deny the thrill of the game, nor could I disregard the financial incentives that tied it all together.

      I sat for several moments looking out into the windy city that blew this clear conflict of interest into my office. It's the same look that I have now, staring out into the horizon accentuated by Hoover Dam and dry mountains. I lowered my eyes briefly to check the time and there lying on my desk was a file folder, labeled "*A.M.*" in bold, black Sharpie. What? How? A moment of simultaneous panic and relief seeps through my skin, as if it were an invitation to something that was both threatening and of great conquest. It's like getting a chill up your spine in the heat of summer. Reports, that couldn't have come from upstairs because I had only been away for a few moments. Someone else was watching me, knew what was going on, and possibly orchestrated the entire thing. It definitely wasn't coincidental that this situation/opportunity was here 9 o'clock this morning, resting comfortably in my office with complementary refreshments before I had even arrived in the parking lot. Regardless, this was my ticket, my advanced level diploma, my boarding pass to luxury, and back-stage clearance to the life I was hungry to inherit. Unfortunately, it also confirmed that there was something happening in this office that was bigger than just me. And even though my dealings with this guy could virtually retire two generations beyond myself, if I got caught I'd be looking at 10 plus years in maximum security. The folder listed counterfeit businesses but truthfully, I had no idea what exactly he did for a living. I thought perhaps illegal prescriptions & narcotics, probably trafficking and street level distribution. But, what if it was worse? What if he and his partners were funding terrorism, genocide in foreign countries, bribed Supreme Court Judges & Congressman, were paying gun-runners, or financing war with US border patrol in an attempt to move heavy white powder through New Mexico? Probably not, but… what if?

My considerations are temporarily interrupted by a subtle tap on the already open office door. It's one of the Sr. Partners and Laurence Baker, the office's Compliance Director. Laurence's job primarily is to monitor the activity of brokers to insure integrity. I'm overwhelmed by an easiness, accompanied by a deep exhale like a chain smokers first blow. He was exactly who I needed to see, the authoritative voice to whom I could release this guilty knowledge of temptation I had been confronted with. I needed to face this. It was the right thing to do… right? That's it! They're both laughing hysterically, probably some internet porn (you could just look at them and tell). Laurence has a seat across from me, and His face changes abruptly, almost as if the warmth and amusement were sucked out of the moment. This dark look overwhelms my temporary feelings of comfort, further compounding what I had already considered a pretty 'heavy' morning.

"Alex…" he starts. "We fight everyday just to compete with big name firms and fancy office views uptown. We fight to have a seat at the table, we fight to be respected…we fight so when people see our name on your business card, it doesn't end up in Lake Michigan! Earning your keep just aint enough… It's your turn Pryce, to man-up and show what the hell you're made of!"

My face is stone, but I still managed a sneer. I don't think I'll ever forget that moment. It's the same feeling that pushes me these days as I muscle my way through the Nevada intensity. Everyday I've got to fight, some days for respect, and other days just to stay alive. But it's an ongoing battle to be recognized in a city that only acknowledges numbers and winners. He stood up, and before exiting he looked at my desk noticing the check which I placed face down on my keyboard.

"…and make sure you close out all of your new business before you leave today, no exceptions!!" The two disappeared around the corner and that was it. I had two choices, I could pack my boxes again, drop that file on his desk, and move on with my life; or I could go all-in! The heck with it, I've got too much pride to be taken for granted again; to be treated as if I'm below the grade, or afraid of the big moment.

This was my introduction to washing numbers, and as part of my education there were specific lessons that I was forced to absorb. For one, when you recognize you're voluntarily involving yourself in something illegal, the manner in which you protect yourself will unfortunately also be illegal. There's no clean way to launder money, and there's no clean way for a launderer to get paid for the wash. It did require setting up a few non-profit organizations, purchasing endowment contracts, creating shell corporations, taking on dependents that weren't mine to set up 529 college plans, overseas Trust funds, Swiss bank relationships, and all other means of moving cash. I even used PayPal a few times! But what made my operation so slick was that most of my accounts were set up for direct deposit within Human Resources. Yeah, you read that right. Doing so meant that I was being what the industry considers "transparent," meaning that the firm was completely aware of my outside dealings, and it could never be interpreted as if I was involved in something that hadn't been approved by my employer. It's all quite complicated, but it meant that I was not creating conflicts of interests in any of my outside business dealings. All of my direct deposit designations had been approved, complete with Tax ID's, and were listed on file. In actuality, the funds bounced around several times before settling in offshore accounts, but the process origin was iron tight. I made friends with the HR Manager, who was getting paid crumbs compared to the rest of us. A few extra thousand cash to support her monthly shoe fetish was a worthy investment to keep the corporate office tied & in pocket. Laurence never even seemed to notice, or perhaps he simply didn't care. We didn't talk, we made money! I figure the roar of 500 horse power from his new Gallardo must have dulled his hearing some.

There also could be no finger prints, so to speak. There would be no signatures, no computer IP address tracks, no initials, no outbound calls, no interoffice mail, no voicemail records, no emails; no trace of my involvement, period! As a matter of logistics, I even started writing with my left hand to create discrepancies in calligraphy. That's the only way I would do it. It required a practice of discretion beyond that of refusing to snitch on connects back on the South Side streets. I didn't talk about my clients, didn't change my appointment habits, or act overly secretive. Nor did I make a habit of not being in the office or slack on my grind. I had to remain business as usual and below radar.

Another Friday, and the first commission check hits from the Moraino deposit. Remember earlier how I mentioned the rush associated with wiring $500K that wasn't mine? I felt that same feeling as cash was instantly being allocated, separated, and moved to about 15 different global designations that only I could access. It was probably the sexiest thing I'd ever seen; six figures resting undetected while my surface net-worth remained middle-class and unchanged. The Partners were so excited about revenue reports, golf club memberships, and new office space near Soldier Field that they didn't pay me much personal attention.

Let's face it, I was making a lot of money, but they were getting filthy rich!

Moraino's next four drops were even bigger, and respectively so were the fee wires. From this client came new ones: product runners, distributors, mercenaries, financiers, and other characters whose work I just didn't want to know about. If I could offer one compliment, it would be that Anthony's crew was extremely thorough. They always used bank certified money, kept to an orderly deposit schedule, even used payroll accounts and fake employee commissions as a means of moving their funds from one account to another. I was earning a first class Six Sigma Black Belt in money laundering, the type of on-the-job training that now proves invaluable considering $31M is a light drop on a heavy Vegas weekend.

More new cars started popping up in the parking deck, especially in the reserved spaces closest to the front door. I knew that his business dealings were a definite inside job, and it wasn't just me who had been tempted to dry clean his particular brand of corruption. And as ridiculous as this whole operation was, I was completely in control and treated his illegal tender with the same respect as the elderly retirement funds I collected uptown. The thrill was as scary as it was exciting. It had become normal to walk in and find cash in my desk drawer or Bulls box-seat tickets taped to my computer monitor. I was even offered a bigger corner office that had the only decent view from the building. But I declined. I never even went to a single game. Instead, I would always shred the tickets twice, and release them out of my car window on the way home. There was no way I'd be caught in an FBI lens sitting in a skybox that was being monitored, or driving a Maserati uptown after the Jazz festival bringing all sorts of unnecessary attention to my self. I kept everything normal, not even a new watch. I donated the drawer-cash to homeless shelters and group homes under an alias, bought books and supplies for my foster mother's students, and even paid the ice cream man to detour his route and give out free cones to kids on the South Side. I didn't need to flaunt bonuses that only make people question what it is that I do, how I do it, & how they can get on! Inner conflict and constant paranoia apparently were my bonus, and it was compounding interest daily!

The most important lesson in my laundering education was the chapter on "Paying attention to signs." I began to notice that the checks were coming downstairs without signatures, were missing bank stamps, and that paperwork was becoming more & more loose & irregular. People around the building and on the Exchange were becoming a little too comfortable in their reclined leather 6-speeds, and it was time to think exit strategy. To me, this was very much a game of timing, just like the main table at Caesars. I couldn't allow myself to be distracted by the dealer's smile, and I had to keep my eyes focused on the table. Signs; it was time to cash out! My mind would drift to a scene at the end of the "Wall Street" flick where Bud Fox is escorted out of the building in handcuffs for taking part in illegal securities practices. Then, it went to "Boiler Room" where the whole crew was hauled off in FBI buses. I refused to walk into a quiet office building with police tearing through my desk files looking for evidence. I would make it count, do what I probably should have done 12 months prior, and get out of the game.

It cost me $20G's but I got my 2-weeks noticed retroactively filed in HR. I stated physical health issues associated with: "Insomnia, assumed to be caused by long nights and levels of anxiety associated with the job responsibilities." Yeah it's a bit of an embellishment, but it was true considering I'd been sleeping in fear for months of either having my apartment raided by the CIA or being associated with the mob! I remember trying to act as normal as possible that day. I took my lunch break at the same time I always did, I chatted about the Bulls with the other broker's at the water cooler, even finished out the week's transaction paperwork as usual. There was no going away party, or a big cardboard box with personal items. I grew up an orphan and thus had no real family to post pictures of, nor did I keep a rolodex of contacts that I hoped to stay in touch with. Even my assistant had quit a few months prior; she also saw the signs. I remember Laurence had taken the day off because the new Madden football game came out. It was some sort of weird tradition that he'd stay at home and let his kids play hooky to play vids all day. I signed out all of my key-cards to HR, did a reboot of my hard drive, and deleted my voicemail greeting. That was my last day... It was a Friday.

I won't get into specifics, and again for the sake of time I'd like to try to move through this quickly. But I walked out of the office that day, just as Anthony had done several months before, fading into the back of the elevator, inheriting the hustler's smirk. Having played my cards, stacked chips, made it to the big boy's table, and cashed out. For several weeks, I don't think anyone even noticed I was gone. It was an implicit understanding that there are no true relationships in this business. My departure only freed earnings to be someone else's eventual curse. It's been several years now and as a matter of fact to my knowledge the firm still hasn't suffered any real consequence a result of their conduct. They eventually moved into that big space uptown on Lake Shore Drive, and continue to flourish. But, the indication that they were becoming lawless and unafraid of making mistakes was warning enough for me to move on. I had earned my cut, and more importantly I had graduated from a real life experience that carried credentials just as heavy as 'Tripp's' Harvard Law, or Stone's Wharton. I walked away having been able to dust away figure prints and any record of my participation beyond a 9am appointment, or a walk to the elevator. But as an entry level, I bleached cash for presumably one of the countries biggest purveyors of criminal activity.

As a CEO, those lessons learned in Chi-Town still apply here on South Las Vegas Blvd: limit risk where you can, ask the dealer to lift the table reserves, go all-in while the table is hot, and retire your knot before the risk gets too high. There is no defending my involvement. I can't simply minimize the significance of not reporting what I knew, of having to funnel cash through multiple streams to protect myself. I didn't concede, instead I outplayed them and withdrew my name from the ballot when the score stopped mattering! With every step, I swept away the trail associating me with that sector; and not only did I clean Anthony's money, but was smart enough to wash my own. I recognized the moment I unfolded that check, that I was guilty of the entire Regulations chapter in my handbook. But I had no loyalties to that industry. Uptown did it's best to make me feel "less than" and the chop-shop forced me to either play ball or box-up my desk. Maybe I was being prepped to be the fall guy, just in case the entire situation went south. The whole thing could have been blamed on the young newcomer who was eager to stack bread and make a name for himself at the expense of the rulebook. Either way, Chicago was rehearsal for Las Vegas sunsets that have reintroduced illegal means of dealing math calculations, and offering legit cash housing to America's Most Wanted. It was a Friday, just weeks before my 28th birthday and I had almost $10 mill buried underground in accounts stretched across the Atlantic. For years, I cleaned crumbs from the head tables of uptown's "Big 5" and in the warehouse district I wiped away more records than Jordan's '96 Bulls… they just didn't anticipate that I'd save a little soap for myself.

• • • • • • • • • • • •

"I had developed an insatiable appetite for the thrill, finding salvation in the hustle!"

Chapter 4: Magna Cum Laude //

I often think about that Friday evening escape. I remember taking the scenic route; driving home with all of the windows down, nodding my head to an orchestra of car horns and laughter of kids headed to the ball game. The Chicago air stream that blew over Montrose Harbor never felt more pure. I had been hazed in a system of unchecked misdemeanors, but I emerged with a deeper understanding of the Dow Jones, as well as an appreciation for what I now call "Liberal Finance." This is when I realized that it wasn't merely the lifestyle I thirsted. In less than a year, I had earned enough digits to live a life of wealth & respectable privacy in the college plains of North Carolina, or even take a 10 year sabbatical traveling the globe writing poetry. I could sale from Montenegro to the South of France, and no one would even notice as I coasted along on illegal tender. It wasn't just the money, because I could live an inconspicuous seven-figure lifestyle just by clearing 10% interest from the portfolio. Instead, it was the love for the game, the sound of the chips, the taste of overpriced cognac... I had developed an insatiable appetite for the thrill, finding salvation in the hustle! Once I finally gained access into 'Freedom,' everything changed.

But understanding it wasn't enough. Hell, I was bored to death! For someone like me, who had grown accustomed to the daily shuffle, I was about to lose my mind sitting around town waiting for the NBA season to gear up. I had lots of clean money I could spend, and I needed to focus on being productive in my professional endeavors... whatever I decided those endeavors would be. I knew what I was good at, but I also knew it was a dangerous game that could not be treated as a simple one-man operation. The alternative was legitimate, but I'd be lucky to collect 1% of what I made the previous year. Transitioning back into what I'd worked so hard to disassociate myself from wasn't easy. But I had to be honest with myself. Fact is, I had no client base and I wasn't connected. I was good at rinsing revenue, but I needed to expand my base; just in case I had to go legit and in an effort to covert ops.

I started attending Executive Education programs in the Ivy League network; Stanford, Yale, Princeton; all the schools we'd beat in conference play. I remember returning to New York for a Columbia seminar, facing déjà vu and memories of speakers who'd brag about the successes that came as a result of their daddy's influence. It was gratifying to have proven the system wrong. To have invalidated an arrangement born in a financial district that eats honorable brokers alive and sends the disillusioned dreamer home broke! I took a tour of the Business School hallways that I hadn't walked in years. It was a powerful moment of self satisfaction. After years in the hustle, I returned to Columbia to accept my honorary accreditations. This simple moment was my commencement ceremony, launching me beyond what PhD students were now being introduced to. My speech was inspired solely by tunnel vision, and a life dedicated to gaining unlimited access to whatever I wanted. I turned the psychological tassel… Magna Cum Laude no less.

I came out of this situation a dangerous recipe for success; like Kettle One mixed with the perfect levels of strength and focus, shaken over ice with a twist! It's no secret; I was feeling pretty good about myself! In an underground sector where even the successful eventually end up on CNN's "American Greed," I felt an undeniable condescension. I networked, joined esteemed organizations, invested in legitimate companies, rubbed elbows with politicians… these were alliances with leverage! I was building the type of personal profile that would've attracted producers of "The Apprentice!" Though my expensive dinner reservations and upgraded "suit-game" were being financed by a past contaminated with bad decisions & sanitized money, the legitimate networks and reputable training programs would level it out. I began to seriously considering tipping the scales. All I had to do was accept mediocrity, long hours, weighted salary, background checks & fingerprint cards, non-disclosure agreements, cold calling, and upper deck seating… YEAH RIGHT!!

I flew up to Boston for a two week Harvard training program. The entire conference was on Compliance Issues; you know antifraud, transaction monitoring, cash screening. Trust me I couldn't make this stuff up if I tried! It was as if the US were supporting my illegal considerations. Between sessions, I found myself lost in the JFK School of Government. Considering my professional intentions to integrate legitimate training with a dissident hustle, I was rightfully displaced. Here I was, possibly one of the nation's most dangerous financiers of illegal bank work, touring the same campus that has tutored several of our nation's former and future FBI/CIA directors. It's like the corner boys who I sat beside in church every Sunday. In their eyes, I could almost read a yearning to find refuge away from their brand of contaminated vending. I never understood their motivation until that very moment, staring in the eyes of monuments whose likenesses embody everything that I respect in terms of leadership & sacrifice, but also embody the regulatory agencies who track my every move.

My first step into the Cambridge courtyard is accompanied by a voice calling out from across the yard, through the deep November chill. "If it aint the Ace of Spades!!" Without even turning to acknowledge, I recognized who it was. Jeremy "Tripp" Starr, III. We played ball together at CU. It had been a few years since I'd last run into him at a random night club in Chicago. We both were hitting on the same girl; shows how some tendencies don't change after undergrad.
"I spent years convincing myself that ghost weren't real. Then, I run into 'Ace' Pryce at JFK? Imma have to go back to counseling because this HAS to be a paranormal experience!"
Same old Jeremy, aint nothing changed! "Just don't tell your shrink about that trip to Puerto Rico, using your experience with the twins as a reference. The way you shot outta that hotel room, I would've thought you saw a ghost that night too!" Don't ask, we were young, baked, drunk off raw tequila, and somehow managed a team of Salma Hayeks when our combined Spanish vocabulary was limited to "Hola," "Adios," "Que?," and "Ci!"

Tripp's one of my best friends, one of the most respected young attorneys in the US, and of course one of my Vegas crew. This guy was born to be great. Both parents, both siblings, ex-wife: all attorneys who graduated from Harvard Law. Of them, he was the only one to be President of the Harvard Law Review. His family's firm, J.D. Starr & Associates, is one of the Nation's most respected and feared in corporate litigation, having settled a $600 million dollar airline dispute just a few weeks ago. They win cases off of reputation alone; an intimidation factor that is calculated into their ridiculously high fee schedule. His grandfather started the firm over 60 years ago, who passed chairmanship to his father. Tripp was being groomed to succeed his dad along side his older sister. But, with all of his family's wealth, prestige, and notoriety Tripp always seemed to reject it, treating it as if he were ashamed. I think that's why we got along so well in college. It wasn't until graduation that I realized how good he had it. I mean, a kid whose father owns a piece of the Knicks, sat nose bleed and ate cheap dogs with the rest of us... crazy. He resented the idea that his life had already been planned, like an arranged marriage or Wrestlemania. When he finally expressed his true feelings about one day running his father's company, the ties were severed and he was exiled into working as a defense attorney in Dade County. The relationship with his father was never the same. His sister is an extremely talented attorney, but as his father's only son the Chairman's desk was supposed to be filled with trousers, not hosiery. His dad is very much a traditionalist in the sense of having no interest in conforming from the "good ol' boy" system. Guess he hadn't quite accepted the idea of a woman's touch in the big office.

South Beach was perfect for Jeremy's personality. This guy would hit on anything with breast and straight teeth (in that order)! I remember him calling me last year to shoot about the Maxim cover and such. Apparently, his office had become the headquarters for drug traffickers and speed boat runners caught between Miami and Havana. He'd developed a knack for exploiting interpretations of illegal search & seizure. In Miami, he had his own Anthony Moraino, drug lords who kept warehouses of coffee and Lidocaine handy for product cover and distribution. So, while I was washing money he was sustaining the industry, performing courtroom CPR in a sort of simultaneous effort to revive his own personal credibility & worth at the expense of the Florida Bar. Sound familiar?

Our roads had crossed; his and mine. Here was one of the country's most powerful minds, abandoned by his family and thus distanced from their resources, all because he wanted to create his own path separate from what we consider "pacifier" success. We both were lectured by Wall Street hotshots who were handed keys to the city. I respected the fact that he refused to just be another "Bruce Wayne." But the decision left him with few options that would compel his father to concede and acknowledge his success. He's established an impressive professional track record. Though it may contradict what he understands to be the truest principles of constitutional law, he still wins cases! Funny thing, the root of his family's acquired wealth goes back generations to 19th century bootlegging, racketeering and of course slavery. "At the *root* of every successful story, there is *soil*;" just enough dirt to make the money stick. Life eventually brings us full circle. So, I never had to propose a partnership with Tripp, it made business sense that we'd merge to leverage the kind of dangerous alignment that taps the US Mint to start printing new money like Hewlett Packard.

Signs… Days pass, and it's my last evening in Boston. Tripp sets up courtside seats at the Garden. How we managed to get better seats than David Ortiz and Randy Moss, I have no idea! At half time, my mobile rings. Of course, I don't have any numbers saved so I lean over to Jeremy "do you recognize this 202 number? DC I guess." That smirk, apparently he's adopted it too.
"It's Stone's mobile… my God! Ace, has it been that long?"
Kyle Stone, one of my fraternity brothers, and current SEC "Broker Hunter." We lost touch after he finished Wharton, mainly because he got a job with the Securities and Exchange Commission. So for obvious reasons I haven't had much of a desire to call this brother. Mainly out of fear that he'd be giving me a warning or instructions to pack a carry-on bag and elope to South America. You know, like in the

"Bourne Supremacy," when he answers the phone and they say "you've got 30 seconds…" or something like that?

"Hello, who is this?" Although we're friends, getting a call from Stone felt like receiving a damn court summons. I never quite pictured him working with the Commission. He had an addiction for tailor made suits, sneakers, and BVLGARI worse than I did! This guy bought Ferrari inspired driving-sneakers in anticipation that he would one day have the vehicle, and thus would be able to accessorize his 430 with tennis shoes. Who in the heck does that?! Nobody, but Kyle.

"Ace, what's up man… it's Stone."
"Stone! Yeah, I'm doing good… uhm, sitting here with Tripp at the game…"

I get this feeling in the pit of my gut, the kind you get right before the rollercoaster dips over the edge and spirals violently downward towards air and concrete.

He interrupts "That's good man. Look, it's been a while, but I need to talk to you. I'm sure… I mean, you probably already knew that I work for the Commission. Well, the Chairman is being forced to resign and unfortunately he's taking my job here at the SEC with him. They're trying to keep it off CNN for a few days, but the guy was taking money under the table, and they're just gonna clean house with his whole staff. I know you're into a lot of different things, and we haven't spoken in about 16 months because of that, but…"

I'm looking around, paranoid. Is he about to tell me that my photo is on the bulletin board in DC headquarters? As I said, criminals are paranoid in nature, especially when you don't have anyone watching your back.

"Ace, I need a job!" Not exactly what I expected. "There's no gratification in opening the books on a firm after they've hustled for 30+ years and made half a billion in the scheme. I'm tired of policing the industry for chump change, just to find out that I was the only agent who wasn't collecting. It's like catching your girlfriend cheating in the middle of the act… you might as well let her finish!"

Stone's the only person I know who would come up with such a stupid analogy.

"Look Ace, I can't talk long, but I'm chillin' right now until I can lock something down. DC was getting too crowded so I opted for a little space. Give me a shout when you get a chance, or maybe you and Tripp can just drop in…" Suddenly, I hear this roaring cheer, and it wasn't from courtside seats responding to lame halftime entertainment.

"Hold on… Stone, where… where are you man?" The roaring gets louder and then…

"BLACKJACK!!"

"I'm in Vegas with Joey Sykes. Stop being cheap Ace, and book your BlueStar! I know you have a private account; don't ask how, but I do! See ya soon."

[Click.]

One criminal defending former teammate; one unemployed former SEC insider frat brother... Right beneath my shades the chips were being stacked. And what if we threw in Sykes? Joey Sykes was a neighborhood kid just like me, moved from the block to Vegas when he was in high school to live with his father. He transferred to Columbia second semester sophomore year to be back on the east coast with his mother after his father was killed on the strip. We were roommates, but more like brothers. His father ran numbers, made sure that certain players won big on the tables, ran strip clubs, had dealers and fighters on payroll… his old man was a street hustler. Sykes got connected in the casino business through his dad's rolodex. Plus, people gravitated to Sykes because he genuinely was a nice guy, the exact opposite of his father. Senior year, he'd hook-up college kids with hotel suites, casino markers, even Showgirls' phone numbers for extra change. It was a crazy hustle, and that was 7-8 years ago when we were kids playing $10 hands in Atlantic City. According to what Tripp tells me, he's pretty locked into the game, and in a serious way.

Signs… This was the type of network that my degree intended to guarantee. Columbia offered connector guys who pretended to have the

President himself on speed dial. It so happens that in our story, we'd create our own luck; success that would propel us beyond the reach of Chicago commission checks, the Dade County DA's office, the SEC Chairman's desk, and even a father's ill reputation.

"...it was like hitting Blackjack!!"

Level Two: Reverse Merger

• • • • • • • • • •

"Ace of Diamonds! Welcome to the Lion's Den!!"

Chapter 5: "Off the Wall" //

"Boeing gassed, bags checked, and I'm airlifted westward into a four hour aerial pursuit of the autumn sunset. The glare seemed to welcome my pending arrival into the desert; from the bitter Illinois evening chill, to 73 degree dusk on the Las Vegas Boulevard."

The Midwestern skies permitted me an extended moment of reflection. For the past several months, while I was either on tour attending seminars or picking up the tab at networking dinners, I'd experienced an overwhelmingly substantive consideration to quit this game. It had been a year since I pushed any form of currency through the Federal Reserve and I was getting along fine, in terms of managing both the offshore cash flow and my very covert image. I could still turn back, reclaiming personal responsibility and honor the warnings messages from foster parents who, from heaven, now monitor my activities with great interest. There'd be no bribing St. Peter; passing through *that* velvet rope would require me to clean myself, not bank transactions. Like I said, there are definite parallels between this style of paper chase, and the kinds that rappers exaggerate over keyboards and bass. I mastered a form of baptism, but wasn't ready to submerge myself into a cleaner way of life… at least, not then.

I've learned to cherish these artless and simple moments, serving as emotional keepsakes of a blessed humanity, however tarnished by illegality. Sure tall stacks of $100 dollar bills have a similar effect. But to recline, airborne at our highest technological altitude, above storm clouds, suspicion, and above fear is Life in its purest form. I still haven't forgotten that one-way flight; the ride and the taste of Louis XIII were so smooth that I temporarily lost track of all grounded concerns; accepting physical and spiritual elevation. I wish I could extend sunsets every evening just like that. These days, I make my strongest attempts alongside an abandoned desert highway just as the weekend begins. But, somehow the sunset always seems to slip beyond the reach of my Aston Martin's top speed.

"That was a very special moment… it was freedom. It was my first time flying over the strip, seeing the Bellagio fountain, looping the boulevard, or surveying the proverbial vault that many have attempted to unlock. The city of Las Vegas feels like it was architecturally inspired by Michael Jackson's "Off the Wall" album! From the sky, the entire strip reminds me of "Don't stop 'til you get enough!" The gleam, the shimmer… I'd never felt so charged!!"

When I touched down, the sun setting over the mountains to the northwest end had a rose colored glow that faded over its peaks like red devil's food cake icing. Considering they encase a strip of concrete & lights referred to as "Sin City," I'd say the analogy fits. It was a beautiful sight to see. I was captivated so, that I began to grasp the state of mind that motivates red-eye flights and daily pocketbook depreciations. It is the Emerald City with an open door policy and free drinks. Today, I speed through this boulevard. But this, my virgin experience & introduction to the strip, was almost spirit led as opposed to financially motivated. I instantly felt at home. Why take a 10 year sabbatical traveling the world when I could get a taste of Egypt, Italy, Rome, and France via limo tour?

I paid my driver to coast for a while. I just wanted to see everything twice; to recap that moment so it would saturate into my mind. Maybe it would decontaminate the ill reputed purpose of my travels. Here I was, once a pour kid whose first Christmas memory was in an orphanage, sharing Tonka Trucks with other boys I didn't recognize. I grew up being shipped from home to home, searching for acceptance and a consistent love that unfortunately didn't come until junior high. With good grades and upon the graces of someone else's charity, I was accepted into an Ivy League network that had been conditioned to neglect the entry of those like me. Graduated with intentions of squeezing capital from the Standard & Poor's, but converged to manipulate acquisitions and deposits of an illegal origin. Clearly my story isn't the conventional American Dream. Yes, I do partake in daily obstructions of justice. But, I made it to a level of success unknown by many, with access to resources people would kill for, corporate potential Monster.com sought after, and a hustle that the Wall Street Journal wished they could document.

"Ace, its Sykes. I'm setup at the center table, MGM Grand. Drop in when you get settled." I'm glad I brought cash! I'm strolling through the center lobby, surrounded by free drinks, "Snake Eyes," and prostitutes hovering over the roulette table like vultures. I haven't seen Sykes since he came back east to visit his mother, who still lives in Inglewood on the South Side of Chicago. I remember we went to the Aragon Ball Room to check out the local boxing talent. Apparently he'd become heavily connected on the boxing scene as well as in MMA, working with promoters to help inflate the odds for potential big fight upsets. We were checking out some new kid out of Tampa he'd brought in town for a Midwestern showcase sponsored by ESPN; a Bahamian Middleweight with crazy hand-speed and a Zab Judah like swagger. That was 2 years ago. Now the kid holds the interim WBC title, and Joey's managing his career full time. He inherited the hustle from his father. Flashy, a tad arrogant; but he managed to sustain a level of humility that came from being reminded of how his old man was found dead in a heap of rattle snake venom and shot gun shells. It's a horrible dose of reality, but it kept the glare of conflict stones from blinding him of the risk associated with his words and actions. He keeps one of the slugs in his wallet as a reminder. This, after all is Vegas… not Mayberry or the Huxtable's Brooklyn Heights.

Sykes was always the life of the party! He worked five jobs in undergrad just to support his Jordan and Polo fetish. As long as I've known him, he's always been the one who everyone wants to get to know, and the one who always buys the first round of drinks!

"Ace of Diamonds! Welcome to the Lion's Den!!" I watched him double-down $35 grand on a 9 of Clubs, 2 of Hearts hand... and hit the Queen for Blackjack!

"Sykes, I gotta feeling we're about to liquidate the entire strip!!"

He's got that smirk; hell we've all got it! It's a contagious quality, brought on by separation from the corporate colony and an introduction to real money. Liquidate... that's what I was there for! All of the awe had subdued, and it was politics as usual as we curl stacks of chips to the cash counter.

"Where's Tripp & Stone?"

Examining the cash stack for accuracy, "They're upstairs. I've got the private room for our usual table setting... you remember?"

That meant No Limit Texas Hold 'em. Me and Ace use to run games with the boys whenever we all got together. It had been some 5 or 6 years since we all were in the same room. Unfortunately, we'd be one man short of our usual, but it was still a stretch to get 4 out of 5. Elevator steel opens to a mob of the most beautiful women I'd seen since the Maxim Christmas party.

"Sykes, I see you still got the inside track!!" There goes Tripp, trying to convince some girl that he drives NASCAR or whatever else he thinks will get him laid... ridiculous! Stone's already trashed and is on the phone arguing with room service, Sykes is pouring Patron like Aquafina... Déjà vu of my college dorm suite, about 7 years prior!

"Have a seat gentleman. Ladies, if you'll excuse us for a little while, we've got some business to line up."

The room empties slowly. "Unfortunately honey, that means you too! Tripp, stop lying to that girl and let her leave! She'll be right back!!" Awkwardly, the suite is swallowed by an unusually tense hush. I think we were all subconsciously sizing each other up. It had been a while, and we'd each changed some. Guys had gotten married, divorced, rich, successful, corrupt... Suddenly, a simultaneous burst of laughter! It was a nice moment, but again one seat remained empty. It was for our 5th, who unfortunately I hadn't spoken to in years. He had gone off to fight in Saudi weeks after receiving his degree. As far as I know, no one's connected with him in years. "$1,000 dollar blinds fellas!"

Just like old times, Joey deals the first hand, Kyle Stone goes all-in without even looking at his cards; and just like I remember he doubles up and folds the next five, talking trash for the next 20 minutes while intoxication continues to set in. Tripp still needs to work on his poker face! The guy has an uncontrollable tendency to stare out of the corner of his eyes, almost refusing to make direct eye contact.
"I fold, Tripp's got pocket Kings!!"
We were the same kids who used to hustle the dorm scene. It's funny to see that nothing has really changed. Sykes has evolved from the campus bookie, but is still a walking Sports Digest. Tripp still tells girls his name is "Mike," and Stone has always gotta start some drunken Republican nonsense to kill the whole vibe. Nothing's changed!

"Fellas, all this is cool… but, I gotta put it out there!" I might as well start it up before I lose my stack to Kyle, who was always the better player. "As always, this is a conversation that stays… what's said here folds & shuffles with deck…" and ironically, it was my deal. "All of us have had a crazy year, to say the least. I'm sure you're all aware of what I got caught up into last summer… and if you weren't sure whether or not what you heard was true… well, it was."
Kyle snickers, as if to write off the notion that my activities weren't news worthy or covert. "Alex, you act like none of us knew what you were doing man! Sykes and Tripp started a betting pool 3 years ago to see how long it would take before my department snatched you up! But I'll admit, you kept your sneakers clean, and overhead at the SEC could never trace your footsteps…"
Interrupting, "yeah, yeah… whatever man. What I'm trying to say is that there are a lot of advanced certificates sitting at this table. Those extras look good on Career Builder, but we're each limited as to how much paper we can make going corporate. I mean, let's be straight. Tripp's got a multi-million dollar client list that stays in court because they don't have anyone to switch out dollar bills. I cornered the Chicago market last year while avoiding wire taps, but I don't have a source. Stone's got the SEC knowledge to monitor the wires and keep us off of the news, and Sykes's can get our deposit into the casino cages and underground vaults… I made

8-figures on the Exchange and never even looked at the Dow Jones. I deal in real money boys… I need to know if you're in."

"Ace…" Joey intrudes… "We all appreciate you taking the time to write that speech, but…we've already talked about this and…" He reaches into his jacket pocket and hands me a key card. "Hell, we've already got a few thousand square feet of office space for covert ops! So, I guess that sort of means," pushing his chips to the center of the table, "I RAISE YOU!!" Just like Sykes to steal the spotlight, I should've seen this coming. "And besides, Mr. Kyle Stone here needs a freakin' job! He's gotta stack a few notes so he can get his own place man. I can't take it no more!!"

It was like when Tripp and I ran into each other in Boston, and when the SEC Chairman's desk changed nametags & Stone had to move on. Call it divine intervention. It was something that went unsaid, that obviously was being considered before I arrived. I didn't have to convince these boys of the risk, nor did I have to sell the reward. Our common link has always been that we were about making money. If we wanted to maximize that effort, there'd be no better way than to pull a 'Teamsters' and unionize.

An elevator's chime overlays drunken laughter and a haze of Sol Cubano cigar smoke. My back is turned to the entrance, assuming a woman's touch from the Showgirls who apparently had been…… Everyone's expressions are still, like when I hired that stripper for Tripp's 21st birthday, and she put a coke can… well, use your imagination. The memory is interrupted by a brash utterance, "Now, how did any of you boys think you'd get rich without the muscle? I mean, can any of you punks even grip a .45 without dislocating your shoulder or passing out?" My head drops to the table, stunned that I even recognize that raspy voice. The empty chair… our 5th!

"'Ready!' Boy I thought you were still searching for Osama, blowing up huts, or whatever my tax dollars are going towards!!"

'Ready' was a star on the wrestling team at Brown before transferring to Columbia. He got kicked off the team in DC for slamming his coach during practice and breaking his collarbone. He had major temper issues; correction: he "has" major temper issues. This guy was either going to be in a maximum security facility or in the jungle sniping terrorists. Good news for society as we know it that he walked into a recruiting office. The military became the perfect place to let loose some of that tension. Marin Corp, special arms tactics, surveillance; I learned that he even did a brief stint with the FBI post Afghanistan.

"Where have you guys been hidin' this boy?!"

"He's also former Director for RVQ, a security company responsible for monitoring casino floor activities and betting cycles…"

"Yeah, that's how Sykes and I hooked up. He was out here buying Pit Bosses and I was monitoring the floor action. When Joey came across the screen, I agreed to conceal the action for him, and of course he commissioned me a piece of the profit."

Talk about needing someone to make sure we keep our names off of police & agency wires. But he also got into gun running on the side, which means he can basically pilot anything that moves and fire anything with a trigger safety. Considering everything that needs to stay clean, we had to have someone who wouldn't mind getting a little dirty. And just like that, we had our Starting Center.

"Look, I've got several business covers, so we'll transition a few of those shells to Vegas. We'll run legit for a while, then Tripp will bring some biz from his South Beach connects. I'll push it through the Federal Reserve, overseas, Dow Jones, etc. Sykes will connect us with the casinos so we can leverage funds there too, just to keep the portfolio diversified and to benefit from the quick draws on fight night. Stone, you'll need to set up surveillance to watch the SEC, Fed agencies, Banks, and whoever else you're still linked into to make sure we're righteous and our faces stay off the wire… The dollars will swell, so you have to make sure the streets are clean before, while, and after we move. 'Ready'… u still got them AK's? We're gonna need you make sure the devil keeps his distance. We'll be managing criminal dollars, so put a small crew together to safeguard the nest."

Pushing a middle-class salary to the center of the table as a point of symbolism, I take a serious look at my crew. "Looks like it's time to go all-in boys... Joey, get the shot glasses!"

That weekend, we partied like we were kids! The crew was together again, accompanied by our total disregard for cost and the legal alcohol limits. We had access to the entire strip with no restrictions. Fights, parties, high stakes gaming... I can't remember much but I do recall getting sick from calamari, and Tripp telling me that I almost vomited Grey Goose on paparazzi that were taking photos of Kobe Bryant entering Magic's after-party... True story! Joey on the other hand passed out at the bar, and had to drag himself back to his suite, barfing "Hulk" every few minutes! Come to find out, his limo driver was a part-time celebrity impersonator, and in a drunken spasm Joey was somehow convinced that he was Hulk Hogan! Literally, every time he tried to tell us the story, he threw up! I mean, who throws up to the tune of "Hulk" every 5 minutes!? It's something we teased him about for months!!

That night, I accepted my inheritance. Las Vegas signed over fiduciary responsibility of its future assets to our consortium, placing me in charge of managing the strip's future revenue stream like an installation of QuickBooks. All future large cap deposits of a questionable nature would filter through 5,000 square feet disguised as a legitimate S-Corp, just blocks from New York, New York. Like I said, it was "the proverbial vault that many have attempted to unlock..." Only difference was, Sykes got us all key cards and we now had access.

"Don't stop 'til you get enough!!"

. . . .

"Like I said when I was recruited for my first bleach, "there was no denying the obvious."

Chapter 6: Smokescreen IPO //

OK, this is how it works: The only way to be an effective cash-cleaner is to have a real, "everyday" corporate cover. Forget what you see on television. You know; Primetime Saturday nights, Crocket & Tubbs leveraging low-level South Beach moneymen to get close to the higher ups? It's nice for a story line, but to be a successful financier of illegal activity, you have to be a legitimate financial businessperson. Windsor knots, pearl business cards, office hours, LLC's; that's why we were able to deal numbers on Chicago's north side and avoid federal indictments. We operated under the cover of what was legitimate, licensed, registered, credible, and more importantly a government regulated business front with highly accomplished personnel steering the helm. Even while we exchanged dirty dollar bills for cleans ones, perceptually we were no different than the corner Scott Trade. Our first moves on the strip were very calculated. We had to prove that we were non-threatening to the culture of the boulevard, like any other group of unknowns who were visiting for the World Series of Poker or Cirque du Soleil and decided to stick around. Any credit union teller can swell a checking account or intentionally misplace a decimal point or two. A true launderer can inflate numbers and receive the "Businessperson of the Year" award.

"That piece of information is free; the next one will require a deposit & completed financial assessment."

But anyway, on to the Initial Public Offering (IPO)… there are five basic principles. I'll try to move through this quickly.

First things first: Legalize. We setup the umbrellas, which are the shield corporations that would protect and screen our illegal outfit. I had a few shell companies from the Chicago jobs that were used to funnel commission checks through the Caiman Islands. Stone and 'Ready' vetted them to make sure they wouldn't show up on any agency radar. Once we were in the clear, I resurrected a few of those and organized smaller business divisions of various diversified focuses. You know, consulting, finance, compliance, management; the key areas which we had practiced professional discipline became part of our new enterprise. All of this might sound a little boring, but it only reinforces my point about having a pro cover. Otherwise, you're just 'some guy' with a hype computer and no alibi. I simply transitioned ownership from me to new tax ID's where corporate power was shared amongst the five of us, making both the risk and reward fairly disseminated. I admit, Joey reserving office space was a nice touch; but I went ahead and bought the whole damn building! That way, we could regulate and monitor everything from phone lines, FedEx, & housekeeping to security guard applications and the maintenance man. Last thing we needed was for the FBI to setup surveillance one floor beneath us in a Travel Agency or a freakin' Starbucks. Besides, it was a good investment. Las Vegas real estate was limited and a north boulevard structural purchase wouldn't attract any unnecessary attention. We had employment packages with retirement plans, full benefits packages, paid vacation; we even had annual corporate "team building" retreats to Rio, and Trinidad for Carnival.

We did business under the associative name: "The Exchange." We were after all brokering crime, manipulating interest, and exchanging currency! We determined price, elevated demand, restricted investor participation, and of course our operation worked in conjunction with the global financial market place. That name cemented our purpose. Amazingly, with such an economically motivated business arrangement, we all accepted the risk without much of a second thought. Nobody turned cheek & walked away mid stroke, or cashed out after the first million. Our team didn't require regulatory tutorials, nor did we need the industry compliance CE credits. We recognized that we were probably being watched, and we anticipated that things would eventually become a little more complicated. But what mattered most was that we were methodical in our approach, that we kept our mouth's closed & weren't afraid to plead the 5th if necessary, and that we didn't go overboard with the personal spending. From our vantage point, it was only banking; just perhaps an alternative to the traditional cash handling system. We were just like all of these other financial institutions that didn't have branch services or drive through windows. You know the ones who offer higher interest rates on their CD's & savings accounts in exchange for your acceptance to 1-800 customer service instead of personal advisers? We were the same, accept it was an illegal financial service… a service that I mastered in the Midwestern banking district; that Tripp defended in court; that Stone investigated with the SEC; that Sykes' father died trying to break into; and that 'Ready' vowed to protect this country against! From the moment we pushed all-in, we knew what we were signing up for. Like I said when I was recruited for my first bleach, "there was no denying the obvious."

Second: Set up surveillance. We kept the office building fenced in tighter than the US Embassy in Cuba! Individual power sources for each floor level, infrared lock-up, camera systems with night vision capabilities, 'Ready' even upgraded the windows so the FBI couldn't use lazar monitoring technology to bug the office. This guy got his hands on stuff that I didn't know existed, like PC's with encrypted hard drives that would melt upon typing an incorrect pass code. The top floor requires voice recognition and pupil scanning to access, and has heat shielding wall monitors to protect against Thermal Imaging Cameras (whatever those are). All of this combined with a personalized security system like the one he developed for the Luxor, an underground panic room, and hired former-military to survey the landscape like clockwork, we were virtually untouchable. But, if it weren't for an extremely high utility bill, there'd be no real visual difference between us and the Bank of America building down the street.

Third: Get some heavy security to go along with the cameras. 'Ready' brought in some additional personnel for security… including these crazy chicks from Guam who had tempers just as short as his! I mean they all could've been fashion models if it weren't for the fact that they used to traffic dope, were hit men, studied torture methods, and did all sorts of other weird stuff. You wouldn't look at Koryn, Lola, 'Quest,' or Jayda and think they'd instigate bar fights for fun, but… it happened a few times in Tao night club. I remember the USA Men's Junior National team thought they were special last summer, and Lola put one of their Small Forwards on injured reserve. They ran rifles & rocket launchers for spare change; and even trafficked gems outta Sierra Leone when it was convenient. I mean, you've gotta be a bad chick to run guns in exchange for conflict stones, especially in Castro country during the Bush Administration. Best thing about it, they were so sharp that they easily could double as evening companions, drivers, even salaried office managers and no one would even notice they were… well, psycho! With all of their nonsense, four-letter language, and tendency to expense Louis Vuitton like lunch, what they provide is essential to our operation. They developed an exit strategy that has become as much an emotional necessity as it is a business practice. To confuse the three-letter agencies, we bought identical AMG's and parked them in the underground deck. So if the streets got hot, 15 Benz's would split the scene while 'Ready's' technology melting all of our office records. It was bigger than the money. Besides, with the bills we were putting aside, I could spend generations in Brazil listening to Sinatra's 'Ipanema' and let the FBI comb through incinerated laptops.

Fourth: Get organized. After the office was setup, we each dropped a few bills into several corporate accounts for smokescreen. Tripp was already licensed to practice law in Nevada, while Stone ran compliance and became our shield. Because he knew where the Fed had a tendency to look for financial inconsistencies, he made sure the books where always clean. The SEC was always welcome to check our manuals. Vegas kept us busy enough to make money without the wash. Stone now plays golf with the Nevada Secretary of State on the weekend, so apparently we're pretty dialed in! Joey began putting in lots of face-time with casino concierge and managing directors. What my rolodex was on the east coast, his contact list was on the boulevard. Treasure Island, Rio, Planet Hollywood; this guy was like a living breathing application of

Google Earth. He knew everyone's name, where they worked & lived, what they liked to eat for dinner, which bar served their favorite cocktail; he was the strip's Wikipedia! My role on the other hand was simple. I was mapping out soft spots and partnering banks whose global market influence kept us out of the news. London, Dubai, St. Kits; this was very much a game of Tag. The key is to make sure that the cash doesn't rest but for a few seconds before it's tagged and released back into cyberspace and headed to the next financial institution. I had several thousand maps, which worked like connect-the-dots as money jumped from place to place before it ended up wherever the client requested. Shake that with Manhattan hedge fund managers who I flew into McCarran pretty regularly to switch out their dollar bills, and the strip had several million reasons to accept our business on their high stakes poker room floors.

Five: Get connected! It's amazing how you can find useful information just sitting around the house. From an old subscription of On Wall Street magazine, I pulled a list of clearing firm that would hold the deposits. Clearing firms are NASD housing bases, and is the core of how your local broker can accept multi-million dollar deposits without having a bank vault. Considering there are only a handful of firms that are capable of, and accustomed to holding the type of dollar action we'd be managing, we might have to work around a leash issue. So, we organized a completely independent biz like Citi Group. Legitimate business accounted for about 20% of our overall portfolio, which today still brings us plenty of work… but of course wash projects didn't ride the books. Most were bleached overseas, so it was pretty easy for us to keep everything separate. Even some of our projects that were semi, we still sent them abroad, to completely segregate our business dealings.

Tripp flew east to Miami, to draw up flight plans and assess laundering needs for the Esés he had been defending in court. As far as I know, he'd never met the boss who was financing all of the action, but he had been defending mid level movers, so there was a lot of money coming through the Dade County ports. 'Ready' even had a few boys he knew from Iraq who connected me in the Middle East. It was risky, but once the money touched desert sand, the US government instantly lost track and had no record of the transfer. Fox News makes it sound like they were public enemy number one, but those guys were experts at covert money movement. But we had to make sure they were priority number one on the books. Those boys would sit across the table from you with C-4 sewn in the lining of their jackets as a warning not to play games with 'em!

Then, the lever triggered jackpot! Sykes infiltrated a few of the smaller gaming hotels, and got them on board with a new scam. Instead of pushing all of our money through the banks and Virgin Islands, we started moving client digits through casinos. It was a perfect alternative. The laundering client swallowed the casino loss like it was our normal transaction fee, and on a fight night, big cash drops would blend in like every other deposit. The casino wash came with a 75/25 split on the transaction fee, so hotels walked away with a quarter just for permitting a weekend deposit, a little table action, and an outgoing wire transfer first thing Monday morning. Here's how it works: if $10 million dollars is spread over 10-12 casino floors and is dropped into the casino cages on Friday night, we charge 10% to launder the funds. That means, we collect $750K, and the casinos walks away with the $250K split. Now when that $10M turns to $250M on fight night, the financial incentive for casino management and pit bosses to push the deposits through are amplified. We were quickly becoming the most connected group on the strip. 'Ready' started offering consulting services to the other casinos that coincidentally weren't receptive to the idea that we were becoming as influential as we were. Unfortunately for them, he worked for us! So, while he was making them feel safer, he was delivering us blueprints, employee logs, and salary information that proved to be good info for floormen who are under paid and over worked. We could double a manager's salary all in one night, and we guaranteed to do it at least once a year. Like at the tables, "money plays" and we had several connects in pocket.

Deposits, laundry, payment, cash flow, and pay outs; our budget books looked like the Yankee's payroll! Considering the level of legitimate business we were doing in Vegas, within a year we each had nice little $3-4 million dollar annual pillow. We decided, no matter what we'd max at $5 million each per year, the rest went into the Bahamas, British Virgin Islands, and other offshore accounts for cover. Too much success brings Feds, envy, newspapers, and unrealistic expectations that eventually lead to reckless business decisions. Stone kept the SEC dancing like the Julliard, and our books were so tight that he was being asked to consult & train other compliance officers as to how they should manage their own books. Go figure, a criminally inspired practitioner of shifting cash was teaching future Merrill Lynch compliance managers how "not to do" what "we do!" Joey headed up the management division and was always throwing parties for his fighters. Tripp became a guest professor at UNLV, and… I was still sending money home to that same, small Chicago orphanage that took me in; just as I had done years prior with bundled cash I found tucked away in my desk. We had so many different credible and legitimate income streams, that the FBI couldn't really identify an entry point. It was like the glare that invited my aerial approach to a Las Vegas runway several months prior. It seemed so pure, so easy, that I felt no guilt in my actions. We were coasting, being pulled along by 500 horse powered exotics and hotel managers whose personal ambition kept us rich and our clients happy.

"Because even with over $81 million stretched from Beijing to Portugal I felt that I deserved more… well, I guess there's also the 276 ft. of steal docked afloat on the shore of Monaco, so perhaps that's $97 million stretched…

• • • • • • • • • • • •

"The winner's circle is the Hefner Fantasy Suite at the Palms; and yes there are champagne baths and confetti showers of various currencies."

Chapter 7: Money Gram //

"Money moves!"

Like when your neighborhood broker advises a change of assets in your portfolio, and he refers to the individual financial products as "Investment Vehicles;" yeah, money moves! And if cash is the medium of transportation, then we are its chauffeurs; safely accompanying digits from the DA's office, to the New York Stock Exchange, and then to the main table at Caesar's; with the same speed and consistency as the Andretti Racing Team. The internet superhighway is our Indy 500; "the boys" are my pit crew; greed is our fuel; and the Federal Reserve is the proverbial green light. Minus the sponsorship tags, we managed to muscle our way through checkered flags & the US Patriots Act. The winner's circle is the Hefner Fantasy Suite at the Palms; and yes there are champagne baths and confetti showers of various currencies. It became academic, sort of like the listening exercise we played in grade school. You remember when teachers would line us up, whisper a message in one kid's ear, and he/she would then pass it along to another, who'd pass to another, etc.? Attention to detail, an intense practice of discretion, trusting what you are told and exercising fluent delivery of financial information… it was just like that. We just needed to be seamless in our correspondence, reject carelessness, & be distinct with every movement. If we did, we would all come into levels of rollover transfers that would finance thousands of square feet with Italian Marble & images by Andy Warhol.

Much of this venture's success is due in part to our ability to simplify the deal. I've seen launderers detox because they refuse to acknowledge the ever-present need to quote- unquote "check 'themselves!'" Greed, lust, envy… Sure, I'm a practitioner of illegal activity and I've made millions of Pesos in support of drug trafficking and violence, but there's a breaking point to which I'm forced to exercise a bit of humility. This is an industry saturated with decisions fueled by ambitions that cannot be achieved. It's like wanting to touch the hot stove, or feeling that 15,000 sq. feet just isn't enough for one person. Money, pride, power; evil is present in everything that we do. Even financial offerings that support righteous social causes are generated by an illegitimate profession. Those who don't last in this business are eventually baited by unnecessary risk, which leads to marked bills, wiretaps, and undercover investigations. The truth is that inevitability is never far beyond the alarm clock buzz. Each morning only promises another day where it could all implode. Those of us who are fortunate to stay fresh do so by accepting these things. The key is to play the dealer, not the player across from you! It is very much a game of blackjack. Success is determined by our ability to keep count, know when to go all-in, and more importantly know when to walk away. Some chips you just have to leave on the table for others to fight over. My philosophy is to simply play to get back what I've lost from the house, plus interest. As soon as the hand turns or you lose the blackjack count, walk away!!

Last week we had a client who needed a little over $20 million cleaned & moved from Maryland to some place in the Caribbean. They flew into Vegas by private jet, made a big scene at the airport because they were given the 2006 Escalade instead of the '08, and wanted to travel the strip via motorcade, inviting all sorts of unwanted attention like they were the freakin' Ambassador of Heroin. Jayda was watching from McCarran International, mentioning that several black suites and undercover earpieces were in the lobby with no apparent place to fly. We got this client on the horn, and cancelled his business while he was still sitting in the Lear pouting about SUVs and hotel reservations. On approach was another plain instructed to take him home. I sighted that there were several security measures that had been breached, and apparently someone in his crew was talking. Of course his boys were fuming! They aren't the type that you want to bark accusations towards without proof. But, I didn't need it! Fact is, 'Ready' cited the CIA had been monitoring his every move, including his flight into Nevada. 10 minute delay, flight departs and lands 75 minutes later in downtown Los Angeles. Landing gear is accompanied by a brief call request to leaves the cash and wiring instructions on the jet.

"We'll take it from here…"

'Quest' and 'Ready' emerge from the cockpit, having piloted him and his crew away from what was a basic government exercise and military squeeze job. This is an example that sometimes you have to practice discretion against the very ones you're being contracted to launder for. That's just the way that I operated, and besides a clean dollar is very much worth an evening of inconvenience. He got over it; they always do. To them it was still like dropping shirts & ties off at the cleaners. An entertainment itinerary, suite reservations, Lakers tickets, transportation for the weekend… man, I even reimbursed his reservation at the Wynn via Money Gram. So like I said, he got over it!

There are a few basic ways to clean bills. Some clients simply want to get their money moved, meaning cash has already been deposited, but they need someone to oversee transit of the funds to another country, to either avoid taxation or just to stay beyond reach of the CIA. These aren't particularly difficult. Periodic deposits, payroll, wires, etc. To manage the work flow, we set up 'OPTION' programs so clients could simply identify their servicing stage by number, like they were ordering fast food. This was an OPTION-1. Just move the cash from this shell account to a bank in St. Lucia where they can actually touch it, spend it, buy more of the product, or finance their choice of corruption. These are my favorite types of deals, because it's easy to extract our fees out during the shuffle, confirm receipt of funds, wipe the trace clean, close up the decoy accounts, and still make it to the Main Event before the American anthem. These are your hedge fund managers, private equity firms, sophisticated white-collar criminals, and a few Washington lobbyists who have a little something extra on the side to wet their appetites for lavish summer beach parties, and Hamptons bragging rights.

Then there are those who only work in cash. These tend to be drug pushers, gun runners, traffickers, buyers who move product from Nicaragua through San. Antonio, etc. These groups have bags of money with no legitimate covers, and no banking relationships where they can make drops & avoid waking the Feds. Let's face it, you can't just go into the bank and deposit $500K in $10 dollar bills. It simply draws too much attention. Even if you consider yourself smart and own several night clubs, cleaners, auto shops, rental properties etc., $50M earned in the entertainment industry is unheard of unless you also peddle clothing and studio films. And of course, these cats want to do business in person. This can be an issue, because as you can imagine their level of paranoia is annoying and of course they're a bit skeptical about letting someone baby sit their money. So, we gotta explain the process, how long it will take to complete, who's involved, etc. But, we never do the same wash consecutively, so we're constantly having to reinvent how we: (1.) get our hands on the cash from the client, and (2.) transfer small bills to large ones. But there are rules to this game. For me, we never meet face to face more than once, no exceptions. If this means that they take their business elsewhere, that's fine. Chances are, these guys are being watched, and though we may be under someone's binoculars ourselves, there's no need to build a joint FBI file just because someone wants to feel special. It's like the Chicago job. I learned from Anthony Moraino that details aren't necessarily the essence of doing this kind of business. He didn't want to know what was happening, and didn't need to know who was handling the deal. He just requested the initial introduction, made an on-the-spot decision as to whether or not he would proceed, handed me the check, and faded away behind elevator steel. This was how I did business, so you get the pleasure of meeting us once, just so we can scout, scan, and complete due diligence. If you pass, we'll accept the deposit and in a few days you'll have new currency. If not, you can take your biz to South Beach and let the Panamanians fight over it.

The first OPTION-2 came about 6 months after we opened. The client landed and immediately wanted to begin calling us to coordinate visuals. Its no secret, the federal agencies pay close attention to the first phone call made on arrival. It's like a jealous girlfriend; I mean, who wouldn't get suspicious if she saw her man calling a random chick minutes after getting in town. Fact is that we knew when his plane landed, how many bags he brought, where he was staying…Sykes even knew the chef that had been assigned to work his reservation! There was nothing about Vegas that we couldn't find out. On the way to his suite, Koryn did the "bump and slip," dropping a 90's style pager into the jacket pocket of one of the middlemen. 'Ready' messaged to confirm arrival via a series of numbers; which could be anything from an address, to desert latitude/longitude coordinates. We put them on the clock to arrive with cash in hand. This is how we worked. Considering the effort we put into protecting our office building, there was no way we were going to be done-in by a tapped line bugged by some rookie agent. It's all about knowing your client. This guy was flashy, loud, Russian, and loved being seen. There was no question he was under FBI surveillance. We monitored their entire road trip, with vehicles switching every few miles just to make sure he wasn't being followed. We locked in binoculars to watch from about a quarter of a mile away, just to make sure that everything looked clean. The slightest inconsistency and we'd walk away. That was the rule, and everybody knew it! We had Malibu money stashed away, and weren't hungry for new business to the extent that we'd risk what we had for a few extra digits. The exchange is made; money for an account number where the funds would be deposited and a confirmation date. That was how we did it. An offshore bank opens a few mornings later, and everyone's happy.

But then there are the occasional OPTION-3's. Some business we'd actually have to consider going after. I mean, thoroughbred crooks who were meticulous in every facet of the game. These usually had both cash & bank transfer needs; but they also had lawyers, accountants, brokers, senators on payroll, lobbyists supporting initiatives that help push their product through customs… These guys did business on speed boats, where the sound of sea and air are so intense there's no chance a wire could pick up convo. They scrambled cell phones within a mile radius of the meeting spot, knew what classes your kids were having trouble in, and weren't shy with threats. These guys were heavy hitters; the cash cows with unregulated wealth and political influence. The experience was elevated not only by their desire to avoid risk in the portfolio, but they were also known to pay extremely well for reasonable rates-of-return. Most clients just wanted to move their cash, or to make dirty money look legitimate. But then, there were the unique opportunities to pick up some interest along the way. Not the type of rates that take a quarter to pay out, or funds that have to be reallocated semi-annually in response to market activity. But the kind of money that jumps and settles in one night's action!

About eight months ago, we went to 'Freedom' to pre-up for fight night. Cyrus Flow, Sykes' Middleweight that he brought to the Chicago showcase, had his first unification title match for the WBO strap. It was a big deal for us to be tied into an undefeated fighter with no holes in his defense and hands like a young Ray Leonard. Sitting ringside, the reading of the score cards introduced an epiphany. Winning his second title made Cyrus the #2 ranked Middleweight in the world; behind Orcrendas Shaw, who had been undefeated for nearly 12 years and had signed to make his US debut versus the winner. Their match-up would be most highly anticipated fight of the year; the biggest name in European boxing versus the fasting rising and most decorated young star since Roy Jones. It was the outage for the OPTION-3 that we needed; the means of generating overnight bill swaps while pushing some growth over casino sports books. A 2-to-1 underdog betting $1M would double his money, or increase 50% if betting on the favorite. All we had to do was make sure that our clients pick the right guy. And that's exactly what Sykes had, a squad of fighters who were in high demand, were highly skilled, gleaming with potential, titlist, young, and undefeated. All of our clients would want a piece of this action, and seeing as how Joey's boy was in-house, it made it that much more enticing to get involved. Thing is, they all wanted to bet the underdog to double up, which was something that we as investors couldn't guarantee, especially considering the records and growing popularity of the fight club. I could monitor a wire to Switzerland via London, Nassau, Syracuse, Tokyo, and wherever else the funds touch before resting in Grand Caiman. But boxing? That money could drop in the casino deposit cage and disappear with an unwarranted low blow or a shifty judge's score card.

The next day, I brought some of the previous night's positive momentum to a blackjack table in the Bellagio. Other than poker, "21" is the only casino game which I am remotely familiar with the strategy. I

lost the count a few times, but I was still having one hell of a table sitting!
Beautiful dealer, Grey Goose Orange & 7-Up… "NICE!!" One of my
fellow players worked at an imports dealer on the south strip; Bentleys,
Lambos, Maseratis, etc. So, I split Aces and hit face cards on the next
turn, forcing blackjack and the dealer to bust! I ended up saving his sorry
14 hand and he added 5-digits to his stack. I remembered watching him
valet the most beautiful sports car I'd ever seen. It resembled a piece of
platinum and sapphire jewelry, twisted around a jet engine. I loaded a
short stack of about $230K in chips and slid it over to him for the new
Aston Martin he was driving around with dealer tags. About an hour later
he dropped the keys off and the valet ticket. $247,350 is still wrapped in
casino tape, stuffed into a Goyard bag and locked in the trunk… the
inevitability of my lifestyle and the "Just in case" stack of hundreds
hidden in the back of a street legal Indy race car.

"SPEEDING!"

• • • • • • • • • • • •

"So while some of us were in class trying to find the lowest common denominator, others were deciphering the metric system & breaking fractions into dollar signs. It never seemed to add up, both in and out of the classroom."

Chapter 8: Addiction //

"When was the last time you "got high? Not in response to an infusion of prescription-less narcotics, but rather had your senses elevated in response to an infusion of reality? Falling in love, Chicago summer Saturdays, that first kiss, Nanna's sweet potato pie, "a perfect day for a ballgame..." We build scrapbooks to capture those moments, so that years post we can double take and still experience the feeling. Because that small dose of realism makes us feel alive, blessed, and maybe even a little lucky. It reminds us that life this side of divinity has an attached expiration date, and we can be pulled from the shelf at any moment. So the question is, "When was the last time you felt high!" When all of the traffic lights were green, when you felt beautiful & carefree? When was the last time you stopped living your live via drive through window, and actually slowed down to taste it? 'High. '"

It is an addictive feeling, to live life closest to the edge where Heaven and Earth seem to meet within ones' self. It is a connection to something beyond price tags and "going all-in." For years having felt neglected, I was finally linked to something that was mine and wouldn't leave. It was success, and wealth beyond nice cars & golf memberships. It was symbolized by $200M cash floating out there somewhere behind vault latches, under sand & ice, beneath concrete, and incased in steal deposit boxes. It was $30M converted into NASDAQ positioned, countered by $25M in international stock options that seemed to overwhelmingly control the global marketplace like Chinese Yen. I got 'high' everyday, and I illegally shared the thrill with whoever had the desire, was willing to swallow the risk, had the layers to endure the syringe needle's pierce, and could afford our ridiculous fee-schedule. It was all I thought about. It became not "how much more can I acquire," but "how can I ensure not to lose an ounce of the servicing supply."

Our dope is washed money. Like some sort of twisted rehab program, I helped criminals temporarily clean their revenue stream. And like LA's young stars, I sent them back into the world, dreading but anticipating a return visit. What irony: to be addicted to an occupation whose operational function is to "clean" or "detoxify." An even deeper paradox is the level at which I was attached to the job. It was I who needed to rehabilitate, just go cold turkey for a few months and let the FBI simmer. But a few months would mean some $20M in Pounds & Francs that we'd surrender, and the dollar was losing value each additional day US troops stayed in Iraq. And even though I despised many of the criminals I worked with, I was no less than what they were. We sold an illegal service, or maybe we just sold clean money. But regardless we peddled what became life support to industries of corruption, distribution, domestic infiltration, illegal disbursement of goods... like Nas said, "*It aint hard to tell!*"

I'm a hustler; it was a desert mirage to envision that I would ever be anything besides that. I forced my way through the khakis, navy-blue blazers, & frat-boy lifestyle, while accepting useful levels of professionalism and etiquette that will forever be apart of my Chicago style. I grew up around street hustlers who saw Al Pacino and the 2nd amendment as their only reliable exit strategy. In the hood, the lights get cut off in one apartment unit, and next door the neighbor is stacking $50's in a shoe box to buy his way into the next big score. So while some of us were in class trying to find the lowest common denominator, others were deciphering the metric system & breaking fractions into dollar signs. It never seemed to add up, both in and out of the classroom. My adolescence was influenced by "Yo! MTV Raps," Sega Genesis, Arsenio Hall, Def Jam, Robert DeNiro, and whatever entertainment was left for me to 'VHS' at the group home. And no, there weren't any doctors or lawyers in my neighborhood. I didn't have a family, so there weren't any uncles who would take me in the office and show me a life beyond the corner, basketball court, and police sirens. It wasn't until I was in college that I found out who my birth parents were... to this day, I wished that I hadn't searched. I was conceived in sin, born then abandoned; adoption agencies seemed to avoid me like the plague… I was just a kid who wanted acceptance, a Christmas gift, and to celebrate father's day. I decided long ago that I'd accept those things that inspired me emotionally; capture them, keep them, and refuse to permit their release. And as the only one of us to survive the streets, I was never able to shake the thirst for *this* American Dream. However for this same reason, I don't visit the South Side except for the Cubs rivalry series. I'd simply be flaunting falsehoods. From a deserted youth, to connected Ivy League professional, to Las Vegas money launderer? Hopefully, there was a new generation of lawyers who would make their way back to the old neighborhood… but probably not.

I grew up in a culture that accepted absence as a way of life. No one seemed to stick around long enough for me to decipher whether or not they truly cared. I lost both my foster parents to natural causes after only a 9 year relationship. Every family before them was just a rental. And as much as I loved the money, I hated that I couldn't share the root of my success with the world. What I was doing wasn't new, and it wasn't as isolated as CNN would like to document. I wasn't the biggest dog in the yard, but I was still allowing myself to be taxed on 7 figures annually, with 500% frozen under French Alps to balance Uncle Sam's withdrawal. It was painful having to hide it, because I wanted to prove to everyone who'd rejected me, doubted me, and denied me that I'd made it without them. I wanted attention to the degree that I would sometimes I feel disrespected if I didn't hear over the wire that our firm was being watched (as odd as that might sound). Trust me, I'm glad that we've stayed above the fray while below camera view, but I have a tendency to feel a little neglected if the FBI isn't parking an unmarked van across the street or taking pictures of the building.

"That's the least they can do!"

I think back to earlier years when I was studying for SEC licensing exams, crammed in 500 sq. feet decorated only with a photo of Muhammad Ali standing over Sunny Liston. To me, that picture is the epitome of strength, concentration, passion, and the ever present underdog's mentality to not just break through the glass ceiling, but destroy the building on the way out! A phantom punch dropped the once dominate heavyweight champion of the world, and the photo shows him searching for answers in the face of an opponent who is younger, faster, hungrier, and louder. "Get up!" That's the look that I fought to capture in the face of government intelligence agencies, Robin Leach, and the boxing promotions groups who'd reject our OPTION-3 infiltrations to swell the odds and layer cash stacks that would require yard sticks to confirm value.

Enter: Krug Rosé, diamond bangles, high society socialites, Paneria time pieces, Victoria's Secret personnel, streaming lights, unlimited access, front row, dark aviator shades projecting through smoke & perfume filled 'Freedom'…

I had finally arrived!!!

● ● ● ● ● ● ● ● ● ● ●

"They don't call Las Vegas "Sin City" to pay homage to street hookers. Loyalties and boulevard affiliations can be bought and traded like cash vouchers."

Chapter 9: Freedom, Aviators, & "Rapid Refund" //

"...Dark Aviator shades project through smoke & perfumed filled 'Freedom'..."

The balcony of club Pure on the eastern wing of Caesars Palace became my refuge. 'Freedom' is where clear perspective is found in the desert breeze. Bacardi O doubles, and controlled substances unearth an alternative personality. Here, I'm in my Zone! The view into the strip confirms Vegas' sometimes reckless vibe, but to me the constant shuffle is part of the city's biology. Pure is just Vegas' DNA spilled over onto day trippers; where licensed bar tenders prescribe cocktails like Xanax, and bar tabs swell like an adverse reaction to the pill. Not quite Chicago summer winds, but still nice. 'Freedom' offers one of the best views of the South Las Vegas strip, mixed with MTV starlette appearances and plenty of VIP privacy for the occasional random hook-up. Friday nights usually end somewhere between the main table at Bellagio and my reserved crimson booth, welcoming whatever worries that may accompany my income bracket.

"The boulevard lifestyle is so Rock-n-Roll!!"

It's the only place in the world where you can assume any identity at no consequence to the truth. Behind oversized lenses, I try to assume normalcy, but arrogance fueled by diamond jewelry keeps me on stage at Tao. Where everyone demands 15 minutes in the spotlight, there isn't another on the strip who epitomizes high-end sophistication and urban swagger quite like me. I blended the South Side's favorite son: Quincy Jones, with the narrator of young, urban life: Jay-Z. Those personalities spiked with a little early Warren Buffet, and the Chairman of the Board himself: Mr. Sinatra, as the twist! Perhaps that's a bit self-satisfying, but that is how I feel. What a wonderful life, where nothing is beyond the extended reach of my personal influence, check book, or corporate jet.

"I remember I'd been in town for almost a year and I still had not seen Cirque du Soleil. The first time I saw it was from backstage, surrounded by props, production headsets, hosiery, and spandex. The next night, I watched as Prince rocked the House of Blues, accompanied by those same elastic acrobats who just the night before, did splits and squirmed beneath fire & electric beams. Later that night we put flexibility to the test, this time beneath silk sheets, the Vegas skyline, and sound's of Prince's "Adore." Again, what a wonderful life, where nothing is beyond my 'extended' reach."

Casino Lobbies vibrate with lever jingles, jackpot chimes, and change machines. There's no freer feeling than hitting the golden mark, and being able to call home and quit your job from the comfort of an upgraded hotel suite. It's what attracts people from Nebraska corn fields and South Carolina beaches. We all desire a moment of absolute freedom from what always seems to be just beyond our fingertips. We work late hours just to be able to splurge on the $800 United Airways business class, a $400 suit, and pocket cash to support the adoption of a new identity. Everyone wants to feel special, desired, requested, and on-demand. Just a stretch of desert, flooded with man made beaches, cash vaults, and an operation that embodies the phrase "addition by subtraction" (considering the losses absorbed just to feel that one meager win to break-even). Because with every bill that we transfer out, we seem to lose a bit of ourselves in the process. Eventually the shuffle machine deals out our fate and the stack either gains, or implodes.

If the boulevard was once considered an untapped flow of green, our business has propelled it to the status of Niagara. These days, I'm just trying to balance the financial variables with reality. You know; the aura of Caesars Palace, and the responsible allocations of presumed retirement? Yachts parked on foreign seas, and donations to support the sinking mentalities of orphans with whom I still feel adjoined? Sustaining illegality, while creating opportunities for future generations? Travels east with global currencies that look like stacks of monopoly money, & church tithes? It's a balance.

And so, OPTION-3's became part of the playbook. For this to work, we had to have several cooperative pieces work in unison. Discretion is our mantra, and is what kept our personal photos off government agency boards. But to infiltrate the Nevada Boxing Commission, we'd need to mix in a few outsiders whose influence we could induce with casino chips and shopping sprees at The Forum Shops at Caesars. They don't call Las Vegas "Sin City" to pay homage to street hookers. Loyalties and boulevard affiliations can be bought and traded like cash vouchers. Everyone in boxing is looking for ways to increase personal deposits, even at the expense of a few pay-per-views and divisional rankings. So, we had to pick our spots, and treat partnership bids like job interviews. But instead of resumes and references, we asked for children's social security numbers and a family photo. If anything went wrong… "God, bless 'em!"

Sykes was not only into the promotions side of the game, but he also had the connections to swell the betting odds in favor of his fighters. This guy managed the spread better than any Options Trader on the open market, bankrolling bookies and odds-makers throughout the strip to keep the numbers balanced. He tends to like the flashy, cocky fighters with the amateur boxing DNA and an Olympic pedigree. And it made good business sense, because even with their Golden Gloves credentials, the casual fan hated their flashy persona and would bet the other way. Flyweight, Bantamweight, Light-Welter & Welterweights, Middles; those were the divisions where lots of overseas currencies were flooding internet sports-books. But even considering the strength of our fight club, there was little room to guarantee financial returns to our investors. And obviously, there are high levels of risk in exposing the portfolio to sports betting… unless we fixed fights.

Fixing matches was like insider trading. We controlled the market place, manipulated the value, and were the only ones who knew which way the money would move. We test-marketed a few ESPN events and Showtime weekend specials in anticipation for the 'Big Score' fight later in the year. Sykes positioned judges, referees, and even managed to manipulate the state athletic commissions. These guys were government appointees who couldn't gamble on fights, so a few hundred thousand spread around to broker score-card decisions would be well worth the cash investment. But we hit the jackpot once we pocketed a few fighters from competing promotional teams, and bankrolled their "simple consideration" to take dives. We couldn't just have our crew losing all the time; it would mess up the money. There had to be a sense of balance in disguising fixed fights with legitimate & fair competition. They were given promises that they'd get a guaranteed title shot against one of our boys if they won the return match, which Tripp always "loosely" wrote into their contracts. All in all, it was an alternative method of cementing the betting index.

Sykes' Management Group became the equivalent to Don King Promotions in the early 90's. We basically had a belt in every weight division. Our corporate logo tattooed the ring apron like the crew from Miami Ink, and we had the power to determine who fought where and for how much! Still, it was a very low key operation. He stayed out of the spotlight, hardly did interviews, and helped all of his fighters transition into legitimate business opportunities beyond boxing. But what separated us from any other promotional group was that Sykes also reached in Mixed Martial Arts, which was slowly cascading boxing's imprint on Vegas sports books & Saturday night PPV's. Before this, the two combat sports were segregated like the baby boomer generation. To say that not everyone was compliant with our arrangements, and perhaps needed a little nudge of influence is an understatement. Lucky for us, 'Ready' and the girls were eager to apply a little muscle when necessary. Waking up in the middle of the night with a pit bull growling at the foot of your bed, and Lola wielding a sniper rifle will make any athletic commission member or ring side judge reconsider his priorities! Simple message: "We can get at you from a few feet, or from a few thousand yards…"

But we only applied the squeeze if they refused to play the game by our rules or we couldn't get to the opposing fighter first. We were fans after all, and weren't positioning these types of opportunities to destroy the integrity of the sport. Besides, fixing matches wasn't something that we'd do often (once, twice a year max). Doubling a fighter's purse just to consider taking a clean hook on the chin is well worth the investment, especially when the contract verbiage guarantees a rematch. MMA was a lot easier to compromise. All a fighter had to do was give his opponent back position and accept the rear-naked choke. Refs, announcers, the fans; no one would ever know. Plus, many of them made little if any money compared to their boxing counterparts. So a suitcase stacked with Franklins and chips from the Wynn was usually enough for a fighter to release his morals, and thus would keep the kennel cage doors closed… usually. Those MMA boys tend to have a tough guy complex that occasionally had to be checked, and my girls loved to "walk the dogs" if you know what I mean.

Once the fight is set, you've got to manipulate the numbers to ensure a spread that's financially suitable. Stone would use his News connects to control the information that was leaked to the betting public. We made up bogus injuries, family issues, nerves, problems making weight; whatever would influence the spread count and push the odds in our favor. 2-1 became 3-1; a 4th round knock-out and $10M spread through the Wynn and Treasure Island turns into $30M. Minus fees, the client clears a 270% flip in one night. Where else can you gain that sort of return on an investment? With the cage deposits secured by management who were now on our payroll, security guards who monitored the cash drops, Pit Bosses who gave us a little action on the tables if we needed to legitimize earnings or show a loss, and 'Ready' monitoring from the casino eyes as an advisory consultant, we had our index finger on the pulse of Las Vegas' Gaming Commission. What a country, gambling losses with laundered money could be written off each April 15th. OPTION-3 became our form of "Rapid Refund."

A few turnovers later, and we were building quite an underground buzz. But because we were so discrete and selective regarding whom we did business with, no one could account for which fights we fixed and which fights we were just putting our own money up. We took intentional losses from time to time, just to maintain balance. Either way it's a tax write-off, so it never really mattered. We began to receive several inquiries from imaginary movers who convinced themselves that they were major players. They'd try to flash a few bills, but that does little to impress a consortium whose combined underground net-worth then exceeded $700 million. I paid $3-4M a year in taxes, just so my operation wasn't so obvious. Why would I grovel at a short stack deposit from an unknown and unproven financial resource? There were business prerequisites and due diligence requirements to be considered for the OPTION-3, and if you didn't fit the bill lets just say we did more than simply reject your deposit!

We had one kid roll in town and immediately began questioning local pros & personnel about our activities. It was obvious that he was either stupid or covering. Koryn hooded this punk in his hotel room, stole the cash load, and questioned him to find out what he was hiding. Like I said earlier, these girls have a PhD in torture, and to her disappointment it only took 6 minutes of acid induced acupuncture before he started talking. His boss was especially thrilled to find out that there was an informant in his crew. They'll never find his body, but Stone still wears his watch to this day. My addiction began to fuel violence, and so it became necessary to subtitle the Vegas welcome sign, warning these young boys that stupidity came with painful consequences. You couldn't just fly into Vegas thinking that we're your average downtown money managers looking to collect commissions and take orders; we were becoming much more than that.

We were on the cusp of something bigger than money laundering. We were overwhelmed with business propositions; transitioning into corporate legitimacy that could only have been introduced via influences of an illegal fashion. Criminal banking was the ticket to the dance. Once admitted, we flirted with real estate, legit IPO's, Limited Partnerships, Mergers & Acquisitions of communications and technology firms, etc. Who'd question us? We were Harvard's, Wharton's, Wall Street's,

Bush's, and Vegas' favorite sons! Even the girls had clean passports! Individually we'd still be rich, but together we orchestrated the commencement of an operational Take-Over. After about 22 months on strip, we introduced a separate financial sector, which in essence is a simple Venture Cap to push our way up the ladder. Simple enough, the appearance was we were trying to squeeze our way into building a hotel properties portfolio like the Maloof brothers. I'd recite my partnership rolodex like it was the Bill of Rights, and ironically to Union officials and Nevada Congressman it was just as powerful! It gave us a backstage pass through corporate & political red tape. We started with a few small properties; nothing big just a few cheep hotels that we gutted and revamped. Flipped those, and now we've got a separate avenue to launder cash through. We didn't want to compete with the big boys, just to collect a few pan drippings while we continue to produce multi-million dollar cage deposits from the Wall Street crowd. Real Estate offered a means of servicing the $5 mill and under laundering jobs. With a 6 month turnaround and liquidity protection, we were investing in residential mid-risers all over the south strip. The word got around, and almost as fast as it would have taken us to complete Doctorates, we had inherited the South Las Vegas Strip.

Today, Aviator lenses have become my disguise, camouflage to the illegality that is now full blown. Behind tented glasses, I'd blend into the Mandalay Bay madness on my way to a ritual Friday evening dinner reservation. A weekend drive to Hoover Dam would extinguish the guilty knowledge of what my job encompasses. It became the preparation point for what the weekend produced. The big deposits were in place, the fighters were dehydrating for noon weigh-ins, the pressure had been applied, and limo motorcades from McCarran International were on approach.

It's like… *"Hoover Dam… at sunset…"*

● ● ● ● ● ● ● ● ● ● ●

"Our service is the equivalent to the purest form of street narcotics; dope with no steps, like dipping a spoon straight into the white package as it's being brought ashore."

Chapter 10: Overtime: "Speeding!" Revisited //

"SPEEDING!!"

Friday's find me East on the 593 to my reserved parking space, amidst Hoover's stone haven in an attempt to distance myself from the strip. The sound of camera flashes & slot machines fade with each manual gear shift, and are replaced with satellite radio & empty highway. Aside from revenue reports and underground deposits that would qualify me for Time Magazine's "Most Influential," my Vegas weekend typically begins with growing sentiments of emptiness. The further I drive from The Exchange office lot, the freer and more satiated I become. East becomes South on US-93 and the emotional contradiction grows even stronger. I've never been one to express religion, but I feel almost spirit led in my escape from the boulevard to Boulder City, Nevada. The more I disregard the speed limit, the less connected I am to the strip. It's as if the Vegas zing is released into the desert air, or is being transferred from the clutch through the speedometer. Donations to orphanages and financing construction for group homes will not erase truths of embezzlement, racketeering, bribery, assault, laundering... even a few pistol magazines that were emptied upon my request. But this drive has had a way of editing my short history, deleting contradiction and illegality from my memoirs. $220 Million offshore, $35 Mill legit, and about $250,000 locked in the trunk. I could just keep driving until I reached Schwarzenegger's constituency, hop a Boeing jet, and escape south to experience Sinatra's "Summer Wind" first hand. The fight deal was in play and the proceeding day's Big Score had been set into motion. Success would put us all over the quarter-billion mark, which would be followed by the inevitable "we gotta talk" moment. When you reach that level, you're either going to back out gracefully, or hire former armed forces to combat vice, SWAT, FBI, and competitors whose clients we were Rolling-Over like old Pension plans. Left turn, and I park.

There'd be no more looking over my shoulder, Cartier disguises, female bodyguards, pit bulls, or distance rifles. There'd be no payroll or prostitution flooded downtown streets. We had positioned ourselves at a level that would justify penthouses at the Trump International Vegas & MGM Residential. Sunsets accompany thoughts of righteous retirement plans; like earlier considerations of poetry in Monaco, and estate planning in the plains of North Carolina. It's the same emotional experience as when I escaped the Chicago Mercantile Exchange; where upon my exit, I settled on about 7-digits cash in addition to an 839 FICO Score. I can still taste that evening's air, feel Montrose Bay across my brow, and hear the roar from Wrigley's upper deck. I haven't had a more pure moment since.

The sun begins to recede westward over what is, with all due respect to the money, responsible for this conflicted lifestyle & Fridays that have me reconsidering. Even the sun seems to be drawn to the "at all costs" vibe of the south Vegas strip. Empty airplane bottles of Belvedere make this process that much more difficult. For months I've been coming to Hoover, but today is the first evening I've actually considered implementing an exit strategy. To truly experience freedom; not just beyond leather booths & nightclub effects, but rather beyond high beams that pierce through the desert distance. I just want to be free! Free of contradiction, wire taps, 40 calibers, and public drunkenness. Moments like these, I'd much rather have public displays of affection, beaches that aren't man-made, a young lady that I could trust with my life, legitimate deposits that don't require bank confirmation. "American Dreamin'."

Perhaps a clearer mind, unaffected by liquid hallucinogen, would have been able to take in the moment and detour a few hours west into LAX. I'm an unregulated banker with numbers resting aside the Great Wall of China, submerged in the Fountain of Youth, and atop Mt. Kilimanjaro. My money was every where and nowhere simultaneously, and there was no way I was gonna fade away before doubling up. In honor of the warrior Joe Louis whose search for acceptance post retirement found him in Caesars, I was going to take back the boulevard, sanitizing both my work and the south strip in one fail swoop. This would be my final trip in search of enlightenment. The next time I saw Hoover, would either be in the eyes of an FBI Agent whose integrity is rooted in the former President's investigative principals, or upon takeoff from a business class window seat.

Bass and Marvin Gaye introduce dusk while alcohol affected hands fumble through navigation switches. The return to the south strip resurrects a reinvigorated hustler's mentality. It is the alter ego, the other personality, the increased intensity of "my zone" that causes elevated speeds onto highway 93 in pursuit of the vanishing sunset. All that talk about giving this up was steadily losing momentum. I felt like I was inhaling exhaust, which from a $225,000 vehicle did nothing but fuel the hustle. It wasn't about the money. It was the "love for the game" that kept me from hanging up the jersey. Fifteen minutes or so, and these towering eyes from a billboard seem to welcome me back home. Those eyes have been the only constant. Mesmerized, and before I know it I once again embrace the vibe of Oz. "Hello honey, it's me!!"

"Valet!!"

Casino lobbies on fight weekends are like mosh pits. Shades welcome concealed acknowledgements from bankrolled Pit Managers, and property hostesses whose smiles should be catalogued by Ford Modeling instead of the Las Vegas Visitor's Bureau. Like I said, "there are too many cameras" for demonstrations or handshakes, so you just connect eyes and keep it moving. On to the private $10K and up seats, to play a few hands with Richmond Kylands, one of Stone's connects and the former Senator of Massachusetts. He's not only up a few hundreds yards at the Blackjack table, but he's on the verge joining the ranks of Clarence Thomas in DC. We met a few years prior at a Harvard U. Executive Education program where he was conducting seminars for students at the JFK Center. A few years later he needed a small financial push for re-election. Our firm bought a few extra seats at an evening dinner fundraiser (well, perhaps a few tables). No big deal! In return he offered promise of an FBI cloak that activates when the President offers him a robe and seat on the bench. Worthy investment, considering his seat will be one of only nine federal positions that are sustainable for the entire life of the individual. So, assuming that he gets the nod and stays away from candy bars, we should be in the clear at least until the next Olympics.

Upstairs to Friday's dinner reservation where I refuel on Merlot and medium-rare. It was happening, and this was sort of my "stop and smell the roses" moment. Tomorrow we'd saturate the boulevard with the kind of assets generated from drug distribution that hadn't been seen in one district city since 1960's Harlem.

"I'd like to extend a toast to the Las Vegas Gaming Commission, the Federal Reserve, the Nevada State Athletic Commission, and the WBO for making all of this possible... Oh, and of course Bank of America for their excellent customer service. Cheers!"

Amidst a personal moment of elitism, I raise a glass of aged red to an empty seat, and exit into the electric wasteland.

South boulevard to Trump International for a change of fitting; Purple Label, Tom Ford, and of course a dark pair of shades to hide sleep deprived vision. My eyes have taken on a crimson, ivory fullness from months of forgoing sleep in anticipation for the big job. Saturday offers a measure of intense conclusiveness, in that it either marks our professional expansion, or possible endorsements of our death certificates. If unsuccessful, the losses of both the portfolio & guaranteed rates-of-return would completely wash away all of my cash savings, putting me back on Career Builder with no valid work history since Uptown Chicago. However a successful implementation would validate our positioning in both legal and underground circles. It was the "put your money up" moment that my executive education experience promised, and would mean a global boom in demand for our illegal stock like Saddam's foreign oil.

And now I'm speeding again north to Caesars Palace. The boys have already arrived, and of course the usual reservation has been prepped. Aside from the Las Vegas Dragons who are pretending to be NFL reserves, and MTV's Reality TV crew; it's a very average 'Pure' Friday night. The private elevator leads to the rooftop, from which I "survey all at which I've manipulate numerically" before fading away into the Red Room. A bottle of Grey Goose Orange is accessorized by a deep glair from just a few feet away.

"Sykes, have you seen her before?"

"Sorry Ace…"

There's something familiar in her face. I feel almost comforted, like Friday evenings when I'm speeding though desert air and new construction sites on the south strip.

"Barman, please send those young ladies…" well, you know the drill. Champaign via FedEx, and shortly afterwards beauty and I are immersed in an exploration of calla lilies & historical coincidences.

"My name is Victoria Ralph… call me Vicky."

From satellite radio, to empty short bottles of Belve, crimson booths in Pure's Red Room, Victoria's approach, her removing my sunglasses in a crowded daze of techno, and finally me removing her La Perla via candle light. Sunset at Hoover Dam later introduced morning by way of room service and Vicky pilfering my favorite pair of shades.

"I'll give these back tonight… ringside, right?!"

I'll never forget watching the sunrise that morning through my suite window. It was the same feeling as when I watched the sun recede on aerial approach, which now seems like an eternity ago. The moment is overcome by and an undeniable arrogance. If you worked as hard as I do; forwent sleep and limited social dealings in exchange for revenue brackets that couldn't be mouthed publicly, you'd be cocky too! This was the leveling point, where years of grind, hustle, and struggle aligned with cash flow & French real estate. The prior day's morning saw fit to permit us to spread 9-digits throughout Las Vegas vaults, and as a consequence the fear of God was deposited in my heart. But I trained myself not to flinch. Even under circumstances like these where success breeds probable government interrogation, my hands must not tremble. The rush of adrenaline seems to intensify with the temperature gauge, and the roar of approaching RPM.

"And now Overtime begins…"

Morning of the Main Event and the build-up has sent shockwaves through the desert floor! I exit street level onto the boulevard, to see my fighter's face on the MGM projection screen just above the hotel entryway: "Orcrendas Shaw vs. Cyrus Flow to determine the undisputed Middleweight Champion of the World." I release the car's rooftop to introduce heaven into what is becoming more and more a spiritually led journey. ESPN Radio is making predictions; my mobile phones erupt with trash talk, v-mail, & text messages; the currency levels in casino cages are balanced to account for the upset; and its not even 9AM! To the Trump for a quick change into old school Ralph Lauren sweats & a '68 Shelby Mustang, just to capture the vibes of the 80's hustler "come-up" infused with Harlem's 70's Heroin rush. Like Nino Brown or Hollywood Nicky; considering tonight's financial take, I might as well play the part! Years prior I found myself mesmerized by this strip of concrete & glass that reminded me of an 80's pop video. Aligning my swagger with the already illegal & underground truth was a simple style adjustment. Tonight, two kids would throw hands to determine the life of 50% of our portfolio. So yeah, I might as well complete the transformation, for one night only, and accept the aura of leader of the new criminal world.

I'm meeting the crew back on the strip for the fight press conference. The lobby at Mandalay Bay manages to sustain the overflow of drunken Brits, intoxicated off of false expectations, displaced national pride, and casino house liquor. The convention center is packed to capacity with English blokes hammering bass drums and singing songs, predicting that their guy's gonna pull off some sort of athletic miracle… wishful thinking. Cyrus is cool though. I mean, he just sits there, not even distracted by the ruckus, chanting, and constant booing from the mostly foreign audience. Trash talk, dollar bill showers, diamonds bangles, Gucci shades; hilarious how this kid reminds me so much of the person I wished I could be in public. But because of my occupation and FBI surveillance, I have to live vicariously through our fighters. Sykes leans in, "I hope Flow slaps the life outta that little prick!" On cue, he doesn't disappoint; palming Shaw's face and nearly pushing him into the front row. I hadn't spent that much time with Flow, but I was starting to love this kid more and more each time I saw him in public. Just that 5 second scuffle probable increased betting on the strip some 10-15%. These white folks hated him, and we loved it because the more they bet the other way, the bigger our wire withdrawal.

The job brought some $250 Million to the table, so it was imperative that we made sure all of the boxes were checked. We spread out the cash deposits over various dollar values and on different days during the proceeding week, just to keep the movement casual. Half of the funds we moved to private cages throughout Las Vegas to bet on the fight. The other bills were transferred through the wire to be exchanged out for clean money. Just like your neighborhood broker, I only exposed a percentage of the portfolio to the high-stakes market. So while half was moving through wire transfers and the casino cages, the rest was churning on & off of exchange floors and through WaMu Free Checking accounts. After the weigh-in, odds for the fight were pushed up to 4-1, which was a ridiculous stat considering Flow was undefeated and brought his own belts to the table. It's amazing how betters wage on emotion instead of common sense. So what if he throws hundred dollar bills in Tao, hung out with rappers, and did a segment on MTV cribs. It's all gamesmanship, and the shit sells tickets. Funny, with all the money that was on the line, I was actually a little conflicted by the disrespect.

This was Orcrendas Shaw's US debut. Obviously from a due diligence point of view, there was no hope of compromising his athletic interests. He was undefeated and had successfully defended his title for a decade without as much as a draw. But let's be honest, this was the case mainly because he had never been tested. He was defending against 2nd rate handicappers & glamorized sparring partners, not to mention fighting overseas in front of his home fans & judges who were afraid to give away a round. He had not however been in the ring against American thugs with fast hands, fur trunks, and Olympic swagger. He would consider himself above our sort of business proposal. Plus, the value of the dollar was weakening against the Pound, so the UK didn't particularly like our money. It ended up not making much difference. It turns out that the referee's mother needed a heart transplant… rather unfortunate. Offering to absorb her hospital bills, on top of a million dollar meal ticket split between one of the judge's and the WBO Supervisor was a small price to compromise the main event. It was an insurance policy, just in case the fight starting getting into the later rounds and our guy had a bad cut from an incidental head butt. That was the only way we could lose. With his athletic ability and our leverage, it was like playing PS3. We controlled every facet of the event, from the doctors to the ring girls. Considering $125 M's were being pushed to $500 mill at a 4-1 spread, and the other $125 Million was being babysat cross country, bribery was just another moving chess piece.

Pitt bosses confirm deposits, hotel managers assure discretion, bookies collect & place side bets, and the girls made sure that the jets were gassed (just in case it got a little sticky). At this point all I could do was wait. For months I attempted to associate a level of legitimacy to what we did. It's only appropriate that we laundered numbers for purveyors of illegal narcotics, because truth is, our job function was just like the drug businesses to whom we supplied life lines. We gave limited hope and distributed clean revenue in exchange for wealth advertised in Rolling Stone and the Robb Report. The operational processes were even comparable. In the drug game, product moves in mass amounts beneath FBI surveillance and Coast Guard radar. In our case, we moved via offshore wire transfers, but it still was an import job. Then product is rinsed a little and mixed to swell the volume. We did something similar, in merging dirty money with legit casino deposits. Next, the illegal prescription is housed & prepped for distribution. Whether it's an abandoned factory, inner city apartment building, or in our case international banks & some 25 casinos through the strip, product placement is essential. Then they cut the product down and dispersed for distribution, like how hotel management and bookies fraction our business into several cash deposits ranging from $25,000 to $500,000.

Pharmaceutical is weighed, cut again, & subjected to street level pushers who fed fiends their addiction and payroll crooked cops to keep vice out of the neighborhood. We write off percentages of portfolio winnings and proportioned losses so the casino would get a share for their cooperation. Alright, perhaps it's not identical, but I think you see my point. Our service is the equivalent to the purest form of street narcotics; dope with no steps, like dipping a spoon straight into the white package as its being brought ashore. Like I said before, brokering illegal finance and supplying street dependencies are of the same criminal species. Trust me, it's not in my best personal interest to glamorize drug dealing, but the alignment was apparent. Not simply in the level of security applied to our bank accounts or due diligence reports, but also in our operational habits. It very simply is who *"I am…"*

Engine revs from the old school Mustang, and navigates me south in pursuit of tailor made accessories. I'm not that disconnected from my past that I neglect memories of my life before all of this money. I remember being deployed from group home to group home, with just two duffle bags and a deflated basketball underneath my arm. I built my wardrobe from hand-me-downs, monthly dry cleaning, my foster mother's sewing machine, and a can of spray starch. I never had the new stuff, just had to do my best with what was given to me. And it might not have been the newest fashion or even a brand name product. But it was clean, and I always had the sharpest crease! Ironically, today I have stylists who respond to house calls and "hand-me-down" customs and exclusives from the runways of designer outfitters. Armani wool blends, Louis, Sean John tailored slim fits, BVLGARI links, Versace, Salvatore Ferragamo, subtle Oyster Perpetual Rolexes of various hues, Valentino pocket squares, vintage Dolce, Alpina aviators… just accessories to a fashionable lifestyle.

Crazy story: I met Calvin a few months ago (like there's more than one) at a showcase to spearhead a campaign for one of his newest fragrances. We both reach for the same glass of champagne, and he turns & complimented me on my style.
"That's a fresh look young man. What inspires your fashion sense?"
"My father, a subscription to Esquire, and… well, you of course!!"

Funny how a kid who grew up infatuated by retro sneakers could receive a fashion cosign from one of the world's most famous designers. Speaking of accessories…

Quick note: girls like Victoria (educated, independent divas who's modeling careers they consider a post MBA coincidence) usually do not answer numbers they don't recognize, so more often than not you should become accustomed to voicemail. This is a problem because anyone who knows me can attest that I do not leave voicemail under any circumstances. On top of that, my number is restricted and set to private. What would you expect? I reposition decimal points for gangsters during my 9-5. One should consider it a pleasure that I'd even save their number in my mental rolodex.
[Ring]
[Ring]
…interrupted suddenly by that laugh, the same as when we sped through the south strip lights into MGM, a vacant elevator, into ecstasy, submerged into intimacy, and finally bubble baptism.
"I was wondering how long you'd pretend like you didn't want to call me boy!"
Perhaps I was acting a little hard. But, I was still trying to fish my way through the previous nights hangover & the multiple orgasms shared between us; not to mention $250 M's & a shady referee!
"If you're still up for it, I'll send a car for you around 6:00…"
That's me getting straight to the point.
"No, I'll be ready at 7:00… I'm at the Palazzo, don't be late!"
[Click]

Now…… Ok. How is this girl going to push my clock back an hour, and then tell ME not to be late? I'm twisted around it because… well honestly… as much as I'd hate to admit it, that's something I would do! Maybe that's why I was so drawn to her. The fact that she didn't need my attention, and wasn't overly impressed by VIP or 62S Maybachs was a huge turn on. I hadn't stopped thinking about her since the elevator closed around her smile earlier that morning. A few hours later and…

eyes, hips, and thighs that made me erect with tension just recapping the night before.

She steps into the back seat Mercedes leather. "I wanna thank the Heavens for the fit of that dress... You look beautiful to me."

From a slim Fendi, she removes a familiar pair of lenses, a keepsake from our previous night's episode, and rests them on her brow. "You mind if I borrow your style to fight the sunset?"

We head over to a Pre-Main Event party in one of the owners' suites.

"Vicky, these are my friends! Jeremy, 'Ready,' Kyle, and... where's Sykes?"

I see Joey posted up by the elevator, taking back a tall glass of scotch like its Vitamin Water.

"Uh, Lola would you mind walking Vicky down to our seats? I just need to talk to Sykes for a few minutes."

Walking over to Joey, "Hey man, what's going on? You look like you're about to vomit "Hulk Hogan" again? Is everything..." His face is just blank, the kind of expression that is on the cusp of hysteria. "What's wrong Sykes?"

"Ace, our ref... he... I... (exhale). I haven't talked to him since we made the quarter million drop to him a few days ago. I think the Commission is going to appoint another ref to the fight, in which case..."

I couldn't help but smirk.

"Joey, relax man... our boy is gonna win!" It was the same smirk he gave me when I first arrived on the strip & lunged into this whole speech about us putting a crew together. "Sykes... 'Ready' locked the ref up in the Venetian this week so he wouldn't be tempted to skip town. Kyran dropped him off at casino few hours ago. He's downstairs man... I guess no one told you..." Like I said, there was no facet of this operation that hadn't been manipulated.

"Now, pull yourself together man, confirm with your bookie, and let's get downstairs before the anthem... Everything's gonna be fine Joey. You trust me, right?

"I trust you... We go way back man... and by the way, you are damn lucky that I didn't see that girl first, because..."

We're sitting 3 rows back; opposite of the HBO camera view to stay off TV & far enough from the ring to avoid blood splatter. We've all seen Denzel's on-screen impersonation of the Harlem gagster, and took notes of the CIA publicity that managed to get him captured between camera frames. No furs, just shades and Armani. I could've been an Oakland Raider or a State Senator for what anyone cared to know. Magic, Oscar, Stallone; the celebrities are out and most are here expecting my guy to get his trunks handed to him, 7th rounds max! It was going to be a great feeling to wipe the shock off of their faces with wagered debits and our newly acquired bankroll. We were looking at complete opposites in the red and blue corners. Boxing's great white hope & Great Britain's king, who was deployed overseas to vanquish the sport's biggest financial draw & its worse marketing nightmare! The build-up was Ali vs. Quarry, post his refusal to enter the draft; or reminiscent of Lennox Lewis' attack on Tyson's untamed alter ego. We inflated the odds, the fans heightened the aura, and all that was left was for Flow to walk through this European nonsense to prove it. The world seemed shocked when he delivered the kind of beat down over 5 consecutive rounds that led to the most academic corner stoppage I've seen since Mayweather Jr. punished Gotti in Jersey. Turns out, we didn't need to payroll the ref, or the judge, or the WBO supervisor. This victory was clean, highlighted by a 5th round TKO and a broken jaw...... it happens.

"Cheerio!"

The market adjusted 400% on our $125M equity investment. The connection of a Joe Frazier like left hook served as our Exchange's closing bell, marking the transfer of $500 Million dollars, earned in 19 minutes of muscle work. Flow unified the division, and in doing so merged illegality and a new found financial credibility on the strip. $500 mill in casino dollars, plus $125 mill rinsed in escrow elevated our team to Olympic status. About $95M in collected fees that we split amongst ourselves and 6-figure payoffs to the moving parts that glued this thing together, plus $12.5M I waged personally flipped itself into $50M... in addition to the rest of my personal assets that were constantly being moved along the Pacific. Looks like I finally passed Sean Combs on the Forbes list.

We were Ivy League, Air Force, Law Review, Washington, and Wall Street smashing Vegas records in a manner that had never been done before. We were America's hope, and its greatest disaster. In one night we tripled the buying power of the world's biggest sources of dope, and we also managed to maintain the same neophyte persona that would finance programs to save kids from a life of crime. The Constitution of the United States encourages safe travels in our individual "pursuits of happiness." I might have arrived during Overtime, but was able to secure one hell of a fashionable entrance!

Level Three: The Richter Scale

● ● ● ● ● ● ● ● ● ● ● ●

"The objective is to get what you can, while it's available… because once CNBC posts and Trump catches on, the Heavies will box you out and move the capital gains to the top shelf…"

Chapter 11: Federal SPF-30 //

There have been doubters throughout my life who didn't think I was ready for, nor capable of demanding the professional spotlight. As a matter of fact, that seems to be the one common indicator of disrespect shared amongst all of us. We were a team of underdogs who developed the dangerous mentality of becoming accustomed to success and winning big. Once we surveyed the landscape, identified our intellectual advantages, demonstrated our worth on the come-up, and separated ourselves from the pack there was no denying our entry. Speaking of worth, in just under 10 years of actual office work and real world experience, I was pulling down Jerry Seinfeld numbers and sitting just a few seats down from Jack at the Staple's Center (to see the Lakers, not the Clippers). It was never about the money, which is probably why I spent so little of it. From a Chicago mid level, I scored $10 million cash and didn't even know what to do with it. Perhaps I was a little overly cautious, especially considering disparity of wealth and access to luxury made it pretty easy for someone to stand out too much. But in Vegas, where you could rent a Bentley for the weekend, and VIP the club scene for less than a few hundred a night, visually I'd blend with the World Series of Poker winners and out-of-towners just looking to blow commissions for the sake of fun. Where else could I collect $250 mill, wash $125M & flip the other half into a half a billion; collect about $95M in fees to split with my crew, and also collect another $50 M's from personal wagering? No other place in the world, but Las Vegas! Atlantic City tried, but they were too close to Wall Street and the SEC. Vegas on the other hand is like Mars to the financial district, is just as corrupt as Congress, and welcomes market manipulation. I'd be remised if I hadn't named our consortium 'The Exchange' considering how we were both the NASDAQ and Dow Jones Industrial Index of the boulevard's financial pulse.

Disregarding the $300M in illegally held assets that were east of the Atlantic, I'd earned over $100M legitimately in real estate and business dealings throughout Nevada. You'd find my name attached to several Limited Partnerships, Board of Directors' seats; this and that. It would take Captain Jack Sparrow to pirate what I'd banked from illegal financing, but the legit stuff was next door in Bank of America, upstairs in the office vault, vested in Microsoft stock, Municipal Bonds, Treasury Notes, and whatever else made me look like your everyday successful investor trying to avoid capital gains tax. I had crazy dough and could purchase anything via quick cash-out. None the less, I still paid a mortgage every month and financed my Benz's. These boys get caught when they go in the bank and pay for $10 Million in real estate with a personal check, or drop a duffle bag on the Manager's desk at the Maserati dealership. If you're gonna drop major figures, make sure they're wrapped with casino cashiers tape, or better yet find a dealer and exchange him a short stack of Bellagio chips (trust me, it works)!

A few weeks after Cyrus won the title, we decided to shut down our shop and take a break. I'd be lying if I said that there were no considerations of walking away completely. Everyone dreams of going out on top, retiring in front of the home crowd, dwindling on NBC with the trophy in hand and personal legacy in tact. There was nothing left for me to prove! I doubled and cleaned a one night order that could've bought the Yankees from underneath George Steinbrenner, and didn't get caught in the process. The firm built its reputation on results, delivering upon guarantees like Ali in Zaire. We were the only exchange in the US that guaranteed interest, security on investment, and timely cash availability. Your broker takes 3 days to confirm cash-out. Las Vegas is a town that operates in cash only, so withdrawals took as long as the money machine needed to shuffle the currency.

But like any other transaction biz, there are always monitors. Don't get me confused with someone who's naïve enough to believe that we weren't being watched. There's little or no way to avoid the administration that was able to capture Saddam and has probably been monitoring overseas phone calls since 2001. $500 million dollars in winnings will get you some attention, and not just from a higher degree of clientele with intentions to infiltrate this country's southern boarders. So, I can't say that I was particularly surprised when my usual Friday evening reservation was interrupted by FBI agents, who decided to raid the dinner table with empty threats and falsified visual evidence.

"Excuse me… Mr. Pryce?"
He waives his badge and sits across from me. Jayda's a few feet away, having a drink at the bar with a silencer tucked beneath a dinner napkin. I shrugged her off; I'm trying to finish my dinner, not start a saloon fight with skinny police.
"My name is Agent Lugar with the Federal Bureau, and this is my partner Agent…"
Well, honestly I can't recall the other agent's name. He didn't say anything, and as a matter of fact he looked rather disinterested. He couldn't keep his eyes off Jayda, who was pretending to flirt just to keep Agent Lugar off guard. You wouldn't think that a Ms. Columbia look-a-like sitting at the bar of a 5-star Vegas bistro would be packing heavy calibers and anxious to let off magazines at a moments notice, but that was her style!
"We need to speak with you regarding some allegations…"
Agent C.J. Lugar: a real prick! Middle aged with a tough guy mentality; the type that we usually had to sick the dogs on.

    "Good evening officers, this is quite irregular but feel free to ask me whatever you feel you need to know."
Whatever man, I'm not scared of the police! It's just like the US enforcement agencies to come around after you've scored and on the way out. Where were you the past few years when I needed an adversary to challenge my economic maneuvers along state lines and through cyberspace? A day late and an agent short!
"I'm going to be direct Mr. Pryce…"
"Thank you," interrupting abruptly, "I'd greatly appreciate that… I'm a busy man."
A little pissed now, he proceeds. "See, I know what you do Alex, you can put this front up for the cameras and the hotel owners who turn an eye to

your dealings because you bring them business, but the US government doesn't work on commission."

Funny, I had Senators, Congresswomen, and a soon to be appointed Supreme Court Justice; all of whom accepted upgraded suits, campaign contributions, and complimentary 'casino play money' in exchange for their willingness to react once I presented myself with a legal issue. I had his superiors on a leash. If that's not a commission job, I don't know what is!!

      "Agent Lugar, kids at Footlocker work on commission. I make cash payments to partners and compensate colleagues via hotel upgrades, dividends, and royalty checks. But for the record, my firm does have a few government contracts… and they pay handsomely. Just so there's no confusion."

It takes a lot of balls to pick a fight with one of George W.'s boys in the era of Guantanamo Bay & Habeas Corpus. After 5 years in the game, I had finally made it on someone's dart board. And as enticing as his apparent challenge was, the fact is that I was fading from the field-of-play to front row seats; from player-coach, to courtside spectator. An image of Michael Jordan comes to mind, '98 finals versus the Utah Jazz, game 6. The perfect crossover, the smoothest release, with his right hand dangling as if he were hanging his divine basketball legacy & second 3-peat in the face of Utah's congregation. It would've been perfect to let that image's caption be the final report on his career. But he had to accept the challenge from players who didn't deserve to share the floor with him. Perhaps in terms of misdirecting decimal points, I'm bit of an illusionist. But I'm a Chicago boy… not a 'Wizard' (if you get my sports analogy).

"Who the hell do you think you are?"

      Like I said earlier, that's usually how it begins. "Agent Lugar, I mean no disrespect… But if there was something that your bureau felt I had done wrong, you would have already taken me in for questioning; in which case I'd be eating mush instead of 5-star. Is it because you know my lawyer is undefeated, that our compliance books are iron tight, that neither wagering nor winning millions on a fighter whom we represent is illegal, or is the knowledge that my head of security is ex-military that's stopping you from making a move?"

He seems almost dumbfounded by my arrogance; clearly he didn't know me well enough. I had no reason to fear the boys in blue. Our work was so thorough, it had never been necessary for me to even pay any of them off! For most, city vice were a necessary expense. For us, they didn't even make it to the 2nd interview! Why fear what has never posed itself to be a worthy threat? It's almost unheard of for a five man syndicate to KO the CIA, IRS, FBI, and border patrol. Pouring himself a glass of wine, he goes on.

"I think you've got me mistaken. You see, I made a nice coin from Cyrus Flow's destruction of that British punk. C'mon son, I'm a fan of your laundering skills…"

"Be careful… And for the record, I don't work at a laundry mat, I'm a banker."

"So, what, you manipulate numbers? Misdirect revenue? Make a legitimate decimal out of garbage money?"

"I'm just playing the game according the unwritten rules of white-collar survival. The objective is to get what you can, while it's available… because once CNBC posts and Trump catches on, the Heavies will box you out and move the capital gains to the top shelf… just beyond your fingertips, where they can control the price and availability… I just create opportunities for others to get involved."

"So, you create ops for laundering clients?"

"No Sir Agent Lugar, I'm not admitting this to be my occupation, I'm just speaking hypothetically…" That's usually how it ends.

He's leaning in towards the center of the table. "Listen Ace, I've lived in Las Vegas a long time. I've seen your kind come and go. The smart ones fly out on Business class into the sunset to destinations surrounded by beach sand & tan lines. You've made a lot of money here… take my advice and cash out before you take too big a hit!"

I reach into my jacket pocket, "Agent Lugar, I own land here, started my business here, and bring in hundreds of millions a year in casino deposits alone. For the record, I determine how the market moves in this city. My firm is called 'The Exchange' for a reason." I lay a few thousand clips inside the bill fold, and a c-note on the table. "C.J., your next drink is on me… and get your boy here one too. He looks like he could use it."

"You know slim, you aren't the first hot shot I've had to visit with. There was a guy about 15 years ago who thought he could infiltrate the strip without heading my warnings, asking for my permission, or even consider giving me a small taste of the gig. I'd hate to have to reload 12 gauges and revisit the rattlesnake ranch."
I halt, turn to confront his open threats with the inherited crooked smirk.
"Rattlesnakes, huh?" (CLICK, CLICK; the sound of a single bullet being called up into a pistol chamber, aimed at the base of his neck).
"Easy Jay!! I'd hate to have to revisit the Governor's Ranch. How would I explain this one?" As we walk away I turn to Agent Lugar's partner. He has no real expression on his face, just eyes that seep a weird sort of indifference and pity.
"I wonder who he feels sorry for."

I told Jayda to alert the boys about the day's happenings. None of us would be particularly concerned with what is equivalent to federal trash talk. For the most part, we worked very hard to maintain reasonably low profiles, kept our personal spending to a limit, paid taxes on all legitimate income; besides a few parking tickets we were as transparent as the funds we dry cleaned. What made us different from crews that either blew deals or didn't implement a strong enough practice of discretion was that we each had a first hand account of the consequences associated with not practicing discipline. 'Ready' hunted and killed vendors of our sort; Tripp fought off prosecution sharks & DA's in defense of them; Stone pursued them via SEC regulatory wire taps; I was on the verge of being posted as the fall guy in Chicago; and Joey's father was found intoxicated in a heap of his own waste and puncture wounds because of it! It's not just about being smart, it's about being disciplined. Submerged in a lifestyle that denounces humility, some have struggled with common-sense notions that sometimes point to early retirement. I made "knowing when to pull out" an art form. It wasn't a bad idea to pull back for a little while; enjoy the riches we'd spent so much time generating, race Ferraris on private

European speedways, and fly east for the Olympics. We had too much legitimate business in Las Vegas to cut ties completely, and I wasn't going to payroll law enforcement who offered no real benefit to what we do. Who care's about one measly FBI agent when I was basically Washington's Head of HR for making side dough! I was all for a vacation! Not because I was being forced out of town, but because I just made $50 mill and needed to increase my overseas real estate holdings.

The doorman at Trump opens the entryway to an inconspicuous arrangement of calla lilies centered in the lobby. Reminds me of Victoria. Night of the main event, we didn't even celebrate with the rest of the crew. We came home early, had my chef prepare a late dinner, savored a few bottles of wine, and just hung out. She was the only thing pure in a weekend driven by transaction covers and illegal payoffs. We spent the evening of my career's greatest accomplishment amidst a candle lit view of the strip, conversing about her life's aspirations and dissertation topics she writes between modeling jobs. I woke up in the middle of the night to find that we both had fallen asleep to the soundtrack of Sadé, & Miles Davis over high def audio. She had to finish her shoot the next morning, and a few weeks later she was business-classed back to New York.

Floral in an empty lobby reintroduces feelings that are independent of the everyday sales tactics I force onto clients at closing. I told her I was in banking. She took one look around at the $8 million dollar apartment, $5,500 suit, $800 bottles of champagne, and said "I'm not one to ask questions, just don't feel like you have to lie." I've dated women who were so infatuated with the view and bar tabs, that they'd forget my first name if it weren't part of the casino hostesses' greeting script. But Vicky I could still feel on my Monday morning pass through of the casino floor. I was tempted to reconvene my Friday evenings with Hoover, just for the return on US-593, and the La Perla billboard that would offer me the opportunity to perhaps rehearse a more formal introduction. I could see why her farther would employ such an emotionally inspired gift to a woman probably of similar style and aura. As Sinatra would intercede, "It had to be you."

Lola scanned the penthouse for bugs, wires; the usual.
Noticing the latest issue of the <u>Robb Report</u>, "Lo, I'm gonna take a little
break from the strip, to my boat in Monaco and wherever else the Spring
takes me. Make the necessary arrangements for tomorrow. I'll see you in
a few months."

A holiday was exactly what I needed. I packed in lieu of a late
summer pilgrimage to figure out the next move; far from Vegas, FBI,
undercover vans, and casino lobbies. But as I dialed into global news
networks to check the climate, I soon realized the measures at which I was
influencing growing international ills. Violent crimes were increasing
throughout the US; Border patrol agents were at war with drug traffickers
who now could afford advanced weaponry; and the National Guard was
actively recruiting young people from the inner cities to battle coastal
breaches that, unfortunately, I'd financed through the spread. CNN
introduced assassination attempts taken against UN leaders; terror was on
the rise in the Middle East; genocide in Asia; gun running through South
America; corruption in Washington; and violence within the war on drugs
just shot through the roof! No matter where I went, I couldn't hide from
my influences. I had to ask myself, *"If it's not about the money, then what
is it about?"* How could I allow myself to be the community banker
within this level of networking? Even my own Vegas streets were
contaminated with prostitution and drug overdoses that could be traced to
my domestic dealings. The game was suffocating me. I needed a new
Friday tradition, perhaps tea at the Eiffel Tower or evening strolls in
Milan.

Suddenly, a buzz from the downstairs visitation desk: "Mr. Pryce,
you have a visitor, a Ms. Ralph here to see you." The elevator opens to
reveal her face accessorized by the same tinted frames she had borrowed
weeks prior, while *her* frame is accessorized simply by a pair of Adidas
track tights, Rainbows, and a relaxed pony tail.
"I wanted to return these before I changed my mind and decided to keep
them. I was in town for a photo shoot… I just finished it up and don't
have anything lined up for a few months. I thought I'd hang out for a
while, no need rushing back to the East Coast… so yeah." This was the

second time this woman appeared in my psyche, then in my presence. With all of the money I made, all of the clothes, cars, and luxury; my portfolio was still incomplete. Its nice drinking from the top shelf, but from time to time you need a glass of water to bring the body to center. She was like water... I don't know how else to describe it. "By the way, did you get my message in the lobby? I thought I'd send you some flowers for the wonderful evening a few weeks ago. I was hoping you'd see them and think of me... The concierge was nice enough to let me position 'em in the front..."

Pheromones release into the ceiling-fan like Sephora is manufactured in the pores of her brown skin.
"Well beautiful, I did get your message. As a matter of fact, that's the first time I've received flowers since my foster parents gave me a bouquet when I graduated college. So, it appears that we both have memories attached to floral arrangements." I reach for her hand and gently lead her inside.
"So, like you said to me... I don't usually respond to these types of things," removing the sunglasses from her expression, "but there's something here, right here in your eyes... I'll sit here all night if it takes that long. This small gesture reaches deep inside of who I am, and I need to know who *you* are." Forever the hopeless romantic...

Tea in Paris, film festivals in Cannes, shopping in Milan, the historical perspective of Rome, and cruise control along the coast of Monaco; Vicky and I spent weeks cramming each destination's respective native tongue on approach, and negotiating the terms of my real estate purchases on the way out. It's like I always envisioned; the freedom to jet-set with one bag in tow, and return with several. A life where I didn't have to pretend to be someone else in order to gain access, or comply with financial prerequisites to be taken seriously. I vacationed several times a day in her laugh, smile, and in the sway of her hips; unexpected considering the haste at which this relationship emerged. I'd only known her for a few months, and I felt dependent upon her presence. Cobblestone streets would offer a blank canvas for us to reintroduce ourselves, and offer the most intimate details of who we are. She'd reveal more about her parents, which forced me to search deeper within myself in an effort to connect, considering I never knew mine. I spent just as much money on Gelato & disposable film as I did on Tom Ford & Chanel. I remember getting caught in the rain while out day-tripping in St. Tropez. We rushed to a side alley for cover, and in a passionate exchange of subtleties we made love right there beneath a tin protrusion & the chaotic downpour. With her I felt such peace, comforted by the distance that had been placed between the Las Vegas strip and this feeling of comfortable complacency.

We spent weeks at sea, parking upon the lip of whichever coastal city we chose. She'd sunbathe from the top deck in nothing but SPF-30 to protect her tone from the torch of global warming. The bareness and freedom of these types of moments make me pity the Las Vegas Boulevard, which at that point seemed light years away. The Vegas streets are always hot, whether it's from blazing desert temperatures or heat applied from the Nevada Gaming Commission. But casino shops don't sell any level of sunscreen to protect me from newly acquired business interests, potentially deadly global clientele, or warnings from corrupt city officers. No FDA approved protection available to block federal indictments, unwanted attention, or ultraviolet rays (or perhaps that's "ultra-*violent*" considering the security measures we took). But, I could just stay here with Vicky. Accept Euros, Pounds, poetry, and the almost $300 million dollar inheritance I buried beneath sea level. Simply dock, fade away into the private sector, and………

"Mr. Pryce, you have a phone call sir. It's your lawyer, Mr. Jeremy Starr."
Just like Tripp to interrupt my holiday. So what, it's been about 8 weeks or so. Get a life man!
"Tripp this better be important, I'm a little busy with something right now…"
"It is… I'm in Miami closing out some of those old trafficking cases in the DA's office, and I met one of the organization's higher ups… and he say's he knows you." Impossible, no one there would know me. I haven't done any business in Miami; Cuba maybe, but not South Beach.

"It's kinda weird Alex, we were talking and… well, he wanted me to just tell you: 'the dice are loaded, and it's your turn to roll again while their still hot!' I'll be back in Vegas at the end of the week. If this means anything to you, you'll be back too."

I temporarily lost the ability to speak, reminiscent of a cold Friday Chicago morning when everything changed. From a yacht deck, I veer off onto the French coast, soon to be faced with tough decisions regarding both the future of our business arrangements, and my past transgressions. After a few moments, anxiety forces a whisper.

"Tripp, pick up some sunscreen… we're going to need plenty of it."

• • • • • • • • • • • •

"Just last night, I was drinking Sangria on black sand..."

Chapter 12: Long live the King! //

The Boeing's descent onto South Boulevard introduces storm clouds and desert rain unlike any that I've seen in Vegas. It's the worst kind, where humidity sucks the atmosphere dry while grey skies leak something that more closely resembles embalming fluid than rainwater. It was like some sort of wicked symbolism as I await the offer to bleach checks like the one I'd received and pondered from a Chicago brokerage desk. I'm now forced to contemplate this type of consideration aboard a private plane traveling westward from European coasts. And so, my conscious descends from sunny skies into a downpour of uncertainty and turbulent conditions. I hated to see Vicky leave, hated myself more for conforming back into what I had evolved above during two months of 'professional leave.' The game just wasn't the same without the trophy, and with her I felt championed by inner successes and the simplicities of just being a young man in love. I wasn't out to get, I just wanted to give; and I was considering giving the crew my letter of resignation to prove it!

If there were a sequel to the film "Carlito's Way," perhaps entitled "The Life and Times of Benny Blanco," its screenplay would be synonymous with Anthony Moraino's wrap sheet. Imagine my surprise to learn that the face of my first bleach job is the boss of street goons Tripp defended in the Dade County court system. This world is a crazy place. The pros in this line of business, I mean those who last and transition their illegal tender into major enterprise investments, are strategic in every move that they make. Anthony Moraino is far too cerebral for this reconnection to have been happenstance. I stopped believing in coincidences after I met Vicky. Anthony is the 'Gordon Gekko' to my 'Bud Fox.' He's the big fish that would be the only client we'd ever need; who would be so tied into our laundering practice that he'd sacrifice guns and muscle to protect our interests from the Agent Lugars of the Vegas strip. We'd exchange clean dollars for leverage. But would that be enough to resist long-term departures to beachfront properties in the Spain?

Success in this business is dependent upon the ability to trust simple principals, one of which being: "Never Look Back!" You have to trust your instincts, and if you're forced to close the books on old business for security reasons, then grit your teeth, and move on! Considerations to plug Anthony Moraino into our client portfolio could be professional suicide, or worse. I shredded the books on his clientele, and disguised my retroactive 2-weeks notice for a reason. Though my decision to move on wasn't directly associated with his inability to practice discretion, the fact is "success is about timing." I flipped his deposits several times over, relocated decimal points like U-Haul, and as a result I commissioned start-up capital that financed my own infiltration of the marketplace. It was a successful Limited Partnership whose arrangement was only to be for a season, at which point separation bred even higher levels of success for both of us. I was already collecting Tiger Woods size endorsement checks and had crushed every long standing record. Encouraging projections showed that I'd earn A-Rod's 2008 salary every year for the rest of my life just from 7% interest, which I could guarantee even in a recession period and with a weakening dollar. I bought 2 homes in Europe, a few more in the British Virgin Islands, in addition to the $20M in full staffed, triple-decked steal that I could dock on any shore that I wanted.

Let's be clear, there was no difference between how I generated my wealth and the American fundamentalist families of old. It might not have been bootlegging alcohol or manipulating the OTC markets, but it was still illegitimate. And like them, I wanted to use my wealth to establish righteous revenue streams, creating generational wealth and opportunity that could be passed on. Send my kids to the best schools; guaranteeing them job consideration and access to resources that would propel them to levels of success I'd only dreamed of. I played the game for legacy, and now that mine was in tact it was time to hang my jersey in the rafters like the Celtics legends I saw when I first considered putting this team together.

"Ace, its Tripp, we're all at the Palms Hotel. Lola's waiting for you at the jet port. Have her take your bags home and come meet us for a drink."
Best thing about club Rain is that the bar is directly in front of the entrance way. Upstairs to the Hefner Lounge, where bunnies deal blackjack and blow dice for $5G rolls. There's a lot of action stumbling through the lounge, which wasn't particularly odd but a bit unexpected considering the weather. The guys were all posted up in one of the side window booths, which was also pretty odd to see considering there was so much young, drunk cleavage in the room.

Tripp has that bad poker face. He keeps his eyes fixed on the inside bottom of his martini glass, avoiding direct eye contact, staring from wall to wall out of the corners of his eyes. We might as well get right to it. "Alright Guys, I'm going to make this quick because I've been in the air for about 10 hrs. My vote is to tell em' we're not interested. We've made millions of dollars by shifting decimals and multiplying deposits. But the fact is that the scene is starting to get a little hot and its time to transition from desk chairs into beach chairs. I know he's got lots of connects, sure we can move all of his money…"
Stone interrupts, "Ace, you've gotta at least here what he's proposing. What Tripp didn't tell you on the phone is that he only wants us to do one job, and not only will we get 15% from it, but he'll pay a quarter above ever dollar on the value of our real estate holdings on the North strip. So, if going clean is what you want, you can do that with your split of the 15% commissions plus flip those raggedy hotels!"

Tripp continues where Stone left off. "Ace, we're talking $500 Million dollars, flipped however we want, in whatever investment types we want, bleached without instruction! We run the entire operation, and regardless of how big a financial boost we create we still collect 15%."
I could do the math. Say we moved through another fight at 3-1, that means $1 billion and some change if we put 75% of it up in cash, then about $169 million in fees, split over the crew with a little sprinkled to staff & bookies would mean something like $32 mill per. Add that to whatever I waged personally, plus the cheap hotels that would go for

$100M mark-up, would sell at $125M as a good faith perk. Easily, it was $100 million dollars, for one night's work.

"I'll admit; the financial specs are crazy. But the fact of the matter is this isn't some simple Tuesday night scratch-off lottery game we're playing! The dynamics have changed. This isn't our first job, nor is this a few months ago when the two biggest draws in sports went head up! Even if we wanted to do it, there isn't a fight out there that would attract the necessary betting volume to disguise our work. And what would we do with the portfolio once he's in it? Once we back out, south strip is gonna be flooded with wannabes trying to vet Moraino, which will make our lives difficult considering our reputation and his bankroll. He'd ruin our legit business prospects trying to bring us back out of retirement once some kids blows $25 mill on a casino scam. That means the FBI starts looking into old jobs, and we're under investigation for going clean! The value of our current book of business just doubled, and our clientele has the cash flow to operate for 3-5 years without another boost. They might need someone to clean it, which is always easier than moving interest or guaranteeing returns. We can do that, no problem. But eventually, as we· grow we have to evolve. Right now, we've got the credit to build a freakin' gaming resort of our own!! So why not go into that biz rather than squeeze a half a billion dollars into 25 casinos, 15 of which would NEVER receive the type weekend volume? I mean, be honest Sykes, who in their right mind drops $10 million in Planet Hollywood? But we'd probably have to, just to keep the tracks clean!!"

I turn to Tripp, who apparently is the leader of this consideration. *"I mean, come on Jeremy. Is any of this really worth it?"*

This is a business, it's not personal. Sometimes you've got to propose the less popular or more conservative road to ensure success. When money's involved, people lose their ability to tap into common sense. No, it's not about Vicky, or Anthony, or Agent Lugar. It's about timing, an element of this business that cannot be ignored and one that I'd mastered. Some people just don't know when to move from cash to checks, from diamonds to debt securities, from the passing lane to cruise control. This was the moment, where humility has to prevail. We are not untouchable, and maintained for as long as we had because we followed the rules of the Smokescreen IPO.

There's that poker face... something's wrong. "Alex, we've gottta do this job. You don't know these people the way I know them. They don't take 'No' for an answer, especially when they make the type of offer they're making to us." Tripp lowers his head, dips into the inner lining of his blazer and removes an envelope. "And you and I aren't the only one's at this table with whom he's familiar." He hands me the package, and I pour its contents onto the table. Out came photos, files, and records of 'Ready' & the girls running guns in South America, and Stone's employment records at the SEC. I'm staring into the lines of these documents, unable to recognize what they mean.
"I'm confused, what the hell is this?"
"He's more than just a drug dealer, he hired 'Ready' to run guns through Portugal a few years ago, which were some of his biggest jobs. At the same time, he was bankrolling immunity from Stone's boss, and was responsible for the whole division being investigated and eventually pushed out. This guy was in business with all of us, virtually responsible for the success we've had in terms of developing our skill sets, and we didn't even know it. Anthony Moraino has been the chief connect for years... and does it from a Vesper on South Beach."

"So what are you saying, this is some sort of threat? Because if it is, it's pretty weak." Pulling a photo from the bottom of the stack, "No Ace, but I think that *this* is as close to it as any."

Tea in Paris, film festivals in Cannes, shopping in Milan, the historical perspective of Rome, and cruise control along the coast of Monaco... There were photos of foreign beaches taken from aboard my yacht, and even pictures of the homes I'd bought along the way.

Attached was a hand written note:
"I've been watching your career with great interest Alex. Now it is time to step up to the big boys table."

At that very moment 'Ready's' answers his mobile; handing it to me. He turns away with an empty look on his face. "Its Lola, she's at your apartment."
"Ace, it looks like you had a visitor at your MGM condo while you were gone." Not possible, visitors are prohibited, especially considering I pay half of the security force to monitor my front door. "There's a duffle bag of shed snake skins and a note. It reads: "Looks like I missed you slim. As you can see, I visited the farm just like I said I would. Perhaps we should try this again... I know where you spend your Friday evenings, so I'll be seeing you soon.""

In baseball, they call this a squeeze play, when the base runner has to make a decision as to which way he's going to go, while each base is being covered defensively. Anthony Moraino applied pressure; wanting me to relinquish hope of a cleaner life. Agent C.J. Lugar presented a threatening opposition on the back end. Like beasts of the Old Testament who were positioned as punishment for Daniel's unwillingness to accept the king's law, this Lion's Den had also been prepped for my demise. Tripp finally makes eye contact, almost relieved to hear the threatening news that has forced our hands. He never had much of a poker face. Confusingly, this expression was always his sign for a bluff.
"Alex, they're looking for an answer tonight. You want me to call him and..."

Disturbed and confused by his level of anxiousness, "No, I'll call... and I'll make contact tomorrow, not tonight. We're not a service that's on-demand!" As I get up to finally head home, there's this weird feeling in my gut. The floor seems to shake, like based turbulence or an indication of a rise on the Richter scale. We had reached another level in our power. It had been confirmed both by threats and demand, reptile casings and illegally acquired background information. We were under attack by those whose overwhelming admiration for our abilities would destroy what we've built. I wasn't going to let that happen, I'd worked too hard for duffle bags and paparazzi to detour our success.

As the club D.J. puts something familiar into rotation, Sykes breaks the silence.

"Do you guys remember that side-bet we made a couple of years ago, that the first person who gives up the ghost agrees to let us play Jay-Z's "Allure" at their funeral?"

Laughing, Tripp lowers his emptying shot glass, "I remember that, "By Request Only" right? Matter of fact, play that and Oasis' "Wonderwall." Just make sure I've got a little house liquor in my casket to smooth out my trip. Whether I'm an old man or…"

Standing to leave, I drop a $50 on table. "I'm not digging my grave yet Fellas. Just last night, I was drinking Sangria on black sand… we'll talk tomorrow."

• • • • • • • • • • •

"It's roulette, in that if you play it enough times the bullet will eventually find you."

Chapter 13: Live Wire //

"Alex Pryce and Associates here to see Mr. Moraino."

I can't remember the last time I made a house call. I hadn't chased business since I was a trainee introducing the "sons of gentrification" to uptown money in Chicago. I'd grown accustomed to prospects swallowing five hour flights west to Nevada, so luxury car rentals and security checks were a necessity that I wasn't used to. And although his proposition was accompanied by a paper trail of blackmail, none of us were particularly concerned with it. Fact is that he's very connected; big deal! We worked hard to have government officials and the up-&-coming hot shots of Washington, DC on speed dial. The entire ride to his South Beach property, I was becoming more and more perturbed at the idea that he would provide bank statements as a means flexing muscle. I falsified numbers for a living, so it would probably be in his best interest to chill on that front. I could flip a $10 dollar bill into a million dollars and deposit it in a Trust Fund shared between he and the Secretary of State. That would definitely be one of my "talking points," like the Senate Committees I pocketed to protect us as we maneuver through financial districts.

As we were being accompanied to the front door I turned and looked at my crew. Most had the same pissed off look on their faces. Maybe it came from seeing my mood change over the 5 hours we spent above ground strategizing as to how we would approach this meeting. We each had a different perspective. I saw it as a 10 minute sit down, where we get straight to the point, hear out the details, make a decision, and beat the sun back to the west coast. Stone wanted to question him. In true SEC fashion he needed details about the dealings that got his boss caught up. Tripp was worried, and surprisingly was showing increasing levels of weakness; perhaps because he was too close to this situation having worked to keep them out of jail for years of illegal activity. 'Ready' figured we should just blow up his car to make a statement. All nice ideas, but it was about business. And so like any good CEO I'd take their thoughts into consideration, but the decision was mine. "Fellas, we're gonna give 'em 10 or 15 minutes… if they aint saying nothing, we're out!"

I've stated several times that you can't be afraid to walk away from business. Professional relationships are just like sexual ones; you can tell as soon as you "go in" whether or not it's going to be worth the time to make it interesting. I didn't care about losing an account. I thought I'd never say this, but *"what's another hundred million dollars?"* I already had about four. Another would still be too much for me to spend in 10 lifetimes. And it's not like I was trying to top the Forbes list or cover <u>Fortune</u> magazine. They couldn't record my numbers anyway, so it was pointless to peak any further than I already had. We were each searched & patted down before his goons accompanied us inside the mansion. We were lead into this huge sitting area with a 15 ft. wall made entirely of glass, which overlooked the oceanic view of the South shore. The property sat on a short cliff, so you could literally stand at the window and see nothing but water and sky.
"No drinks for us, thank you." We were here to do business, not to hit an early happy hour.

"Good Afternoon Gentleman! Alex, it's great to see you again!" Anthony has the same smirk, same gentlemanly swagger with a hint of elitism. Years prior, elevator doors were closing around his words of destructive influence. This day, we shook hands and just stared at each other for a moment. Almost as if it were an English standoff to establish strength, and intimidation. I wouldn't allow fear to be dissected from my gaze. I felt disrespected! With all of the success we'd generated and the means at which I had kept my company off of front pages; the fact that an old client, regardless of how high up the ladder he was, would have the audacity to drop pictures and deposit slips in an effort to pose a threat, angered me beyond words. This was a fight for my legacy, one at which I planned to keep intact. This was Michael dribbling the clock out with the

Utah Jazz scrambling for defensive position, or the fulfillment of Reggie Jackson's Mr. October pseudonym.

"You'll have to excuse me if I'm not as enthused Anthony. It seems that someone hired paparazzi to take an interest in my vacation plans. I take issue with that tone of disrespect. And although I don't particularly follow the regulatory code of ethics, I do believe in honor amongst thieves."
"I just needed to get your attention Alex. I've been watching you for some time now and admire your success…"
Squeezing his palm a little harder, I grin and whisper "well, how about sending me a damn e-card next time!"

His security reaches for hip metal. He's the boss, and I'm sure that no one's ever talked to him that way without having to go through surgery. But the facts were he wouldn't call us all the way East to Miami to tussle, so reaching for pistols that weren't going to be used was just another empty threat.
"Point taken Ace, I get it. Now, please have a seat so that we can discuss business."
Tension subsides for a few moments, and my mentality settles in the aggressive calm. It's almost as if I found comfort in being agitated by this whole occurrence. I had an FBI agent in the city that was trying to crash the party, and Anthony attempting to pressure my crew into doing jobs. The disrespect only fueled my irritation.
"I appreciate your hospitality Mr. Moraino, but we know each other well enough to not beat around the bush. Clearly you've got something big in mind. If you could lay it out for us, we can decide whether or not it's in our best interest to work it." Tripp gives me this stunned expression, like he's afraid to talk. On display is that same weak card face, the kind that puts you on the bench during the World Series of Poker tourney.
"I think what Alex means Mr. Moraino, is that we value your time, and don't particularly want to waist it if it's something we can't handle." If it weren't for a half billion dollars worth of biz and a few people sitting between us, I probably would've tossed him from Anthony's cliff balcony!

"Well," Anthony begins, "The fact is, I've been sending you guys business for years. The only person here that I haven't had contact with in some form or fashion is Joey. I've gotta say, it was genius for the five of you to crew-up and take the landscape by storm. You may not realize this, but you guys have absolutely monopolized the marketplace. Our former financier threatened to put a hit out when he heard I was taking meetings with you." Condescension seeps through his baritone laughter like a desert thunder storm.

"Well, 'Ready' caught wind of that nonsense before I closed the books and went on leave. I'm sorry, but you'll find that his shop is now closed permanently." 'Quest,' & Kyran, paid him a little visit a few days after he went public with his mouth. Now, we don't usually condone involving family members, but he lived with his wife's folks as a cover for his illegal activities. Sad thing about it, his in-laws didn't even know he was funneling cash through their DSL connection! With Mother's permission, the girls let the dogs loose on him in the basement right in the middle of dinner & Jeopardy.

"Now, the details please…"

"What I need is about $500 million bleached, with $100M safeguarded, and the rest I'm willing to accept exposure to whichever market that can push me at least 25% gains. All of my money is cash, literally. So, this will require you to: (1) shrink the bills for me (meaning that his deposit is mostly $5's and $10's which will need to be "shrunk" into denominations of larger bills, so there isn't as much paper to move); and (2) do an on-the-spot wire transfer for cleaning, once I deposit it with my bank…"

Interrupting, "So, you're asking us to shrink, and follow it up with a *"Live Wire?""*

Live Wiring makes the process much more different. Most banks hold deposits over a certain dollar value for a designated amount of time. It depends on the type of deposit (check, money order, cash, transfer, etc.) but it could take weeks before funds are cleared & available. Wires were usually easy to handle, but a huge deposit like this one, dropped at

11:00am in a merchant's bank, then moved to 10 different designations within 30 seconds before resting offshore is like trying to pickpocket a police officer. Advancing bank regulations have made this a dangerous game. It's roulette, in that if you play it enough times the bullet will eventually find you. His proposal was absolutely unnecessary considering we could initiate a "slow burn" strategy and move the money over several months. His actions were the signs of someone who either didn't know what they were doing, or doesn't have the banking connects & correlating revenue streams to cover the cash drops as legitimate income. The whole point of shrinking bills is to make it look credible. For instance, you can't have a real estate development company, and tell your banker that an investor just made a huge cash contribution to the development fund with $20 dollar bills. You'd get locked up just for being stupid!

"So, tell me which is it. Did your banker get arrested, or is your supplier becoming increasingly frustrated with your financial inconsistencies? Because anyone who requests a Live Wire on the first job, not to mention a shrink plus capital gains is either desperate or unorganized. Which are you?"
I can feel Tripp's glair from the other end of the table. Why should I be forced into a situation without being able to see the playing field? "Anthony, I gotta be honest with you. This isn't the type of business I typically am anxious to take on. Also, it's a lot of work that none of us are particularly interested in being burdened with." I get the smirk and nod from the whole crew, except for Tripp who's got this illegitimate responsiveness that's making me angrier by the moment. "Last time we spoke Anthony, you said you were transitioning business. I think if you want us to consider what you putting on the table, the least you can do is give us access. Otherwise, we have nothing to talk about." Something's changing. Even as the dialogue evolves, I'm becoming a bit less conservatory and more liberal in terms owning the tone of our discussions. I remember him coming on my turf and forcing $30 mill off on me like it was loose change. Right now, as far as I'm concerned, this whole deal is just that.

"Alright Alex, you want the truth?" He begins to walk outside, turning slightly to Tripp who's denying eye contact. "Come take a ride with me." We step through the glass door, and down stone steps to the ocean below. We strap into a 377 Talon speed boat, put on the receivers and speed south on the bay. Instead of covering wiretaps in the basement wash room, why not race luxury speed yachts and talk over headsets?
"I didn't want to talk about this in front of everyone; not even my own people know the specifics about what's going on. Truth is I'm financing a global take-over of white powder. We've got acres of product land in Columbia that are being transferred over to us, and I'm just finalizing the buy. I need money to purchase guns, hands, farmers, runners, street men, politicians, and military to protect the location. Don't get me wrong, it's jungle territory, but we need to put workers on the ground. As soon as we buy, our former distributor is going to remove his men from the property and leave it unattended. I've gotta put people there ASAP, so at closing I'm basically dropping off $700 mill in cash and an operation that's ready to strap in."

"Well Anthony, that sounds very profitable, but what you're proposing is just too much work for a five man crew, especially with the type of flip you need just to keep it balanced. Las Vegas can't handle that kind of action. After the hit they've taken from us, we can't put the strip under that level of pressure." Suddenly, he pulls off the throttle. The engine revs violently as we slow to an almost reckless halt.
"Let me ask you something Ace...... How much do you care about your friends?"

My face turns to stone as I snatch the headset off in response.
"Listen, you don't want to play that game. You know what my security ranks are capable of. If you've been sending us jobs, then you're familiar with how my girls are with acupuncture needles..."
"No Alex, that's bad for business. I'm talking about Tripp. You ever wonder why he's always undercutting your authority... Why he's working so hard to try to get this deal in play?"
I never really thought about it, I hadn't even noticed a change in his behavior until a few weeks ago.

"Tripp was here in Miami defending my boys on possession indictments. Then he beat the D.A. on more serious charges, so we put him in line to make some moves of his own. To cut to the chase, let's just say he made some bad business deals with our Columbian brethren. He came in short on some trafficking scams; real short!! Then, he came down a few years ago, promising to flip some money in a real estate project and I took a hit personally. He's been paying his debts off a few of mill at a time. Truth is; we still got over $65 million in credits on him."

"I'll wire it to you tomorrow…"

"No Ace, you don't understand. I've been protecting Tripp for months. Now, my guys want to either see his debt double over, or permanently put him on life support. See Ace…Tripp brought us back together. Having knowledge of my proposal, he figured he could break away easy by making the introduction. It wasn't until he showed me pictures of you on vacation that I even made the connection. Nor had I realized that 'Ready' ran mercenary jobs and Kyle's boss was on our payroll. I knew what you were doing, but we moved on a long time ago. I had no interest in coming back to the table and breaking bread with you again. Tripp is the one who packaged those pictures with Stone's bank records, not me. Yeah, we've all done biz, but the reunion was an inside job."

The afternoon sun began to beat down like the torch of the Vegas Strip.

"Ace, your boy said he'd be willing to double his debt if you weren't able to pull this off… which puts him in the hole $130 million, plus interest. The only reason he's alive right now is because I don't feel like interviewing lawyers. But, even talent isn't worth the heat that's coming down on me from organizations that are sick of him not paying his bills on time. I'm not going to protect him any longer!"

And here we are, floating along, several miles from the coast, surrounded by water and betrayal. Dishonor in our industry usually results in death. Problem is, Jeremy's one of my best friends and I don't think I could face his mother at the funeral. This is why it's a bad idea to go into business with people you know. It introduces an emotional element that otherwise shouldn't be present. Under normal circumstances, 'Ready' would take care of it and I'd never hear the details. With a friend who I've known since freshman orientation, it wouldn't be as easy to place that order. We've joked about "Allure" and "Wonderwall," but I didn't want to personally be responsible for making a request to the DJ.

"I'm gonna be honest with you Alex. If you say "No," when we walk back in the house I'm going to signal & Tripp's brains will be splattered all over the living room wall. And I promise if your boys as much as flinch, I'll wipe them away too. Don't get me confused, I'm sure that each of you snuck a piece past security, so we can let the steel decide it! But, you've got the power to see that all of us walk away from this rich and ready to do business."
How could Tripp do this to me?! After all of the money he's made, $65 million in the red is like breaking a dollar for a quarter! All he had to do was ask for it. I'd rather he owe me than pressure us into owing credits to the Cuban mafia. Now, the South American underworld is holding his debt hostage, using it as leverage against our group for future contracts like IOUs.

The speed boat finally parks along the coast. "So, how are we gonna do this Alex? Are we going to close our eyes and hope for the best, or are we going to make a little money and plan for retirement?"

Sliding glass doors open, and I notice this blank stare in Tripp's eyes, almost in a regretful acknowledgement of what he's done. His head drops in his lap, surveying the room from the corners of his eyes like a coward. He couldn't even look at me. Judas; betrayed his crew just so he could get in good standings with the King.
"Anthony, I'll call you with instructions in a few days."
My eyes turn to Tripp, as do the rest of the boys almost in a synchronized reaction. Some things just go unsaid. We beat the sun back to the west coast, all the while battling the urge to detour the flight plans midair, cash out, and toss Tripp from the cabin area to prove a point.

• • • • • • • • • • •

"So, if done properly, this type of job could be pulled from a Starbucks on a Bluetooth, or from an undergraduate library PC with Skype!!"

Chapter 14: "Offshore Drilling" //

The flight west would be the last time that we would all share airspace. As kids, we'd pack into a rental van just to save money on Spring Breaks to Daytona Beach. But money has a way of switching things around, which was apparent when we could no longer share 'Freedom' beneath night club lighting and the influence Bacardi. We had become victims of our own success, and Tripp's extortion leveraged our services out like pre-paid legal, or buy now-pay later e-commerce. Our due diligence was scrapped, security had been infiltrated, risk levels heightened, all because one of us chose to eliminate his personal debt using an unauthorized business line-of-credit. Our operation survives via an insistent practice of discretion, and now we were offering baseline info to people whose communications procedures we weren't familiar with. A wiretap in South Florida inadvertently records wiring instructions, and the next thing you know the streets of Las Vegas would begin to melt right beneath our feet.

Perhaps the mistake was mine, in making our arrangement an equal partnership when in all actuality we were an LLC with laddered responsibilities and tolerances. Corporations with legitimate paperwork can designate levels of personal liability, stock percentages to dish out during expansion, and organize transferal of power. The underground doesn't work that way. If one person on the team goes down, more than likely he'll bring the ship down with him. The only way to force transferal of power is to arrange a doctor's appointment for the transferal organs, if you get what I mean. Anger aside, we had a job to do; which required nothing less than 100% accuracy or we'd be planning each other's memorial services.

I began to wonder how many of our other deals had been leveraged, and perhaps more importantly, *"why hadn't I caught on?"*

Jeremy was jeopardizing our futures just so he could get his debt out of the red, and I never saw it coming. His pupils looked like cherries, from weeks of sleep deprivation mixed with high blood alcohol levels. Considering the fact that Moraino's crew put a checkpoint on his life, and the way 'Ready' seemed to walk around with death seeping through his expressions, I probably would've stayed awake too! Deceit from within forced all of us into a shared degree of emotional confliction. Along the bloodline, we are brothers; according to the Commissions, we are partners; but, this is an emotionless industry. So our individual fates were merged together like decks in the casino shuffle machines.

It had been weeks since I'd talked to Vicky, blatantly avoiding her calls and texts in an effort to keep her away from this mess. She's the only thing in my life that's pure, and unfortunately to keep our relationship clean I had to separate her from my work. I had the FBI interrupting dinner plans and South American drug consortiums pressuring unrealistic capital gains. Withdrawal was the only way I could keep her safe. And although it was killing me, it was what needed to be done. Days seemed longer, and Fridays just weren't what they used to be. As is a true in any profession, once you grow tired of the daily grind, you either have to find a source of rejuvenation within your work, or find new work! I discovered peace in being a professional vacationer, a lover, a traveler of European seas & airways where currency changed color like Monopoly paper. So, even though it may not have been in my best interest to continue taking my usual evening dinner reservation, I refused to allow Tripp's fear or the FBI to dictate how I chose to partake in civil liberties. I'll admit there were a few evenings I had to bring 'Ready' along for the ride, just to monitor the perimeter while Lola or Jayda kept me company via candle light and 24 carat table settings. Considering my platform focus on issues of "Inflation" & services performed for Cuba that I like to call "Offshore Drilling," (not to mention that I engage in higher levels of International Diplomacy than a Republican Nominee for President), secret service of sorts became a necessary measure.

In order to move Moraino's load, we needed cash available in both high volume & high denominations, to switch-in clean money for street level drug money. I've collected a few bankers over the years, all of whom were eager to earn extra coin levels to buy luxury items that the Federal Reserve Bank system doesn't salary. And while they've proven themselves to be dependable, this was a different type of job; one that required personal oversight. I could not trust deposits of this level to a banker who'd probably pass the drop instructions on to a 22 year old teller. The most efficient approach would be to bypass the investment geeks and link to institutions that would be willing to accept an "as is" deposit. Most banks in today's financial climate will press the panic button on trash bag drops filled with $20 dollar bills. The great thing about Las Vegas however, is that the city will not turn away *any* currency type. Each casino has a private room for the big boys, center floor tables with $5,000 minimums, and penny slot machines. So, all we needed was to mix our deposits with their weekend cash cycle, manipulate the system to disguise our movement as high-roller wire transfers, and run the numbers from the casinos to overseas banks.

Sounds complicated, I know. But all I need is a laptop & high speed internet to pull my end of the job. 'Ready' could get me secure access into their financial systems. From there, I could wire the funds in & out during the "Live Wire" transfers. Considering we were doing everything "live," it was imperative that we move in unison, everyone on the same page and at the same time. Running it this way gave us the freedom to skip the cash shrink. Instead, this was just a laundering gig where we had to personally monitor the drops. So, if done properly, this type of job could be pulled from a Starbucks on a Bluetooth, or from an undergraduate library PC with Skype!!

Percentage points however would be more difficult to dictate. Cyrus Flow was now world champion, and wasn't an underdog to any challenger in his division. So, to generate the type of flip that we did on the first big score, we'd need to bet on his opponents, which for a management team is an obvious display that a "fix" is being setup. We could move him up in weight, but Sykes had this kid's long-term career to consider, and he wasn't ready for that type of push. Besides, this was the type of job that needed to be completed in a matter of minutes. Boxing not only has too many variables, but their start & finish times can't be controlled. A fifth round Knock Out would wipe about 15 minutes for fight intros, maybe 14 minutes of action, and 4 minutes of corner stuff. That's about 45 minutes in between when the bet has to be placed, and when the fight could end, and that's only if the damn thing starts on time! So, unless we could guarantee a first round stoppage and a 7:30pm PST main event start, to work a fight would be pointless. Not to mention, sports-betting was becoming more CNN News worthy. A few college officials got indicted on charges of affecting the outcome of Bowl games, and the Nevada Athletic Commission I'm sure had their eyes on us after a few new Porsches, bankrolled through our last job, began popping up outside of their headquarters.

However, with all of its potential downside, it's silly to ignore the type of volume that big money fights attract. And as we considered easing off the gas to find another entryway, the answer seemingly presented itself to me at a drive-through window (of all places), on the north-end. How many times have you paid for something and needed a penny to square the bill? One cent doesn't make that much of a difference to your pocketbook, but as our currency's lowest denominator, it can be moved inconspicuously and without anyone really giving a damn. And so, the strategy came to me in line at a mom & pop bakery, encrypted on a $5.01 receipt. As an alternative to flipping money in the ring, why not work the casino system against itself and nibble from each wager? The larger casino houses would have some $300-$400 million per vault for a largely televised main event. The way I figured it, if we stripped a penny from each dollar waged on the fight, we could easily generate a 2% total return on the cash drop. For example, 3-1 odds betting "the under" on just $300 million spread throughout the strip, would generate $900 million dollars. If we pulled a penny or so from every, individual dollar bill waged on the underdog, we'd end up with $9 million cash, or exactly 2.25% of the $400 million we were washing in the vaults (excluding the other $100 million that we kept secure from wagering). Two pennies would pull $18 million, or about 5% return on the $400 mill. And if the odds moved to say 4-1, the penny could generate $12 million in returns off of just $300 M's in betting, which would probably only represent a third of the total action on the strip that night. Whatever the numbers were, 3-1 odds on $500 million, or 4-1 odds on $400 mill, or maybe 3-1 on $700 mill total from the entire strip, we stood to make a killing just from stripping cents from a dollar. We could just tag the penny strip as a casino operations fee, and because it's so small no one would even care.

But we had to attract more money than usual, or at least create the "the perception" of more money. First thing was to create the type of hype to grabs the attention of the Forbes lists and high profile betters who had a tendency to flood the sports books. Months prior to flying east, Flow announced that he was considering making the jump to Pro Cage Fighting. ESPN and sports bloggers went ballistic, creating the media frenzy we needed to channel betting volumes that would support the kind of inflation we were going to push through the system. A fast rising Mixed Martial Artist erupted on scene to make the challenge and the game board was set. This is a storyline that you've probably heard before, considering sports has a tendency to recycle the script every 10-15 years. My boxing digest only goes back as far as Ali-Forman, but even then the story in Zaire of the underdog hero was scripted as such. And so, this young kid counteracts the hype and is an instant 2-1 underplay. How the more experienced, stronger, Mui Thai fighter got tagged the underdog, I have no idea. All I know is that it was just what we need to draw the "$20 million per movie" crowd east from LAX.

Sykes' PR connects throughout the strip made contact & booked reservations for about 50 of Hollywood's elite, plus a few ball players; complete with tickets to the fight and whatever else they wanted. He also had a crew who managed the casino floors. They were responsible for letting us know when the high rollers arrived, so "their" check-in times would be synchronized with "our" wire deposits. Then there were my Hedge Fund and Wall Street hot shots from New York, who I flew in to bring credibility to the fluctuation of casino balances, as well as name recognition to the deposits. Since celebrities and VIPs are accustomed to being comp'd and mostly prefer to travel under an alias it wasn't out of the ordinary for them to have reservations under an "a.k.a." This worked to our advantage, considering we could temporarily deposit our cash under the assumed name during the day, and flush it out before anyone noticed. Trust me; if you have a cartoon film that just grossed $150 million in its first week or you were on MTV cribs, nobody's going to question a $5 million dollar deposit and withdrawal on fight night.

Several weeks of planning have culminated once again on a big weekend. Déjà vu; I remember when I'd raise my wine glass to an empty seat praising my own work, and even threatened government agents who interrupted my meal. Regardless of what happens tomorrow, like Hoover Dam I offer valediction to my past which, until now, I haven't been unable to shake. From dinner reservations I managed to relive years of misled potential that through memories I have trouble escaping, even from aboard G4s and a 911 Turbo. Murder, extortion, racketeering, laundering, bribery; all of which could be traced back to the desert I'd inherited in route to the kind of success I'd always hoped for. There'd be no Victoria tonight, just a debate with myself regarding the tax code and whether or not $400 million generated from "offshore drilling" was ever worth the harm it was causing the environment.

"Valet!!"

••••••••••••

"It's your turn slim, to man-up and show what the hell you're made of!"

Chapter 15: "Laundry Day" //

Simplicity is the name of the game, and although the details of our servicing proposals sound more like the Wall Street Journal than a comic book, the base of our work has always been very simple. This particular job however, pressed our discipline to the limit, forcing me to consider unorthodox strategies that were as maddening as they were genius. Then, finally came that Saturday morning, it was "Laundry Day!" Most people would be surprised to find how much money actually moves before their kid's cereal boxes open and Sponge Bob monopolizes the family room television. Today our offices were open, and inside we were preparing for the financial-fix of the century. There could be no mistakes, no hesitation; and if everything worked as planned we would not only be in the upper 8% in terms of net worth, but we would have completely burned this issue between Moraino & Tripp. Today would be his opportunity to prove himself, to regain friendships that have lasted through millions of dollars and a few death threats. After having betrayed those who were now responsible for defending his life, we would have our own personal laundry to air when the Exchange closed.

But first things first: "Take Care of the money!" We had to deposit Moraino's cash into the casino vaults, without anyone noticing. Sounds impossible, I know. But 'Ready' was able to access the casino deposit schedule through consulting jobs he pulled with hotel security. Apparently on fight night, they drop cash first thing Saturday morning, 10:00am sharp. The Armored Car service that had been contracted to handle the drops is owned by a former Marine who served with 'Ready' in the Middle East, so the connection put our guys in line to get uniforms, vehicles, supplies, badges, and more importantly entry through the back with the normal drops. All we had to do was slide an extra few mill in with the normal deposit chain. Once the account balances were adjusted, we'd begin the "Live Wire" transfers. We'd mask the celebrity aliases' wire withdrawals as a computer error, stating inconsistencies between the actual amount deposited and the amount recorded in the system.

Consider this process like finding an extra $600 in your checking account, and then the bank recognize the error and took it out without telling you. Because it was never supposed to be there in the first place, they didn't need to explain it. The same financial principles apply here. The surplus deposit would appear in the system as accounting error. Only difference is that the cash had physically been deposited into their vaults and removed electronically. So, when they release the additional funds, which appear to be simple accounting errors, they are actually releasing cash money; balancing their checkbook via a series of laundered deposits that they never even knew about!

At 9:30am, the cash begins to roll in from highway 593, split just as we had arranged with different designations throughout South Las Vegas. Clock hits 10:00am PST, and the phone rings.
"Ace, its 'Ready,' let's get this over with... Press Enter!"
He gave me this crazy computer that looked more like the Captain's panel on Star Trek than a PC. It made me a virtual ghost, giving me access to the financial networks and making my IP trail invisible. Some crazy piece of info tech like they use in Baghdad to scrambles frequencies. Even from the most sophisticated hacker's screen, my system was impenetrable. I uploaded our overseas account lists and logged into the access points that manage all of the casino records on the strip. This is where it gets interesting. I basically have less than 180 seconds to move the entire amount, in separate increments, over several hundred channels throughout the world, and settle them in escrow. I looked at it like an Etch-a-Sketch photograph, in which I'm the only one who knows the sequence. To everyone else it's just a bunch of lines, but to me it's a piece of art. $10 million through London, Dubai, San Fran, Iceland, Puerto Rico; then $2.5 million through a Credit Union system in Anchorage, Tokyo, Mongolia, Budapest; $17 million straight through the Pacific coast to Peru; and it goes on. I can't really explain how I'm able to move it so fast. Once you've mastered it, it's like playing a computer game. Especially from the Bloomberg double screen monitors attached to high speed wireless.

Before you know it, the $500M is replaced with a zero balance as a computer error reboots the system. And just as I promised, we only exposed 80% of the portfolio to the gaming market and settled the remaining $100 mill in separate account. A mouse click from my computer turns off all of the machines in the network as if there were a mass power override to reboot the system. The lines immediately restart with no record that anyone was ever linked. Just normal administrative screens to check in guests, normal security points to monitor betting cycles, and the usual financial screen to oversee accounting. I confirm that the numbers from the deposit match what should be in the vaults, and initiate the self destruct mechanism in my hard drive.

"Simple!"

All of our VIPs had checked in on Friday, which gave us access to some 65 aliases spread throughout the strip. We'd only need to attach $6 million or so per name, but of course with some of our players being on the Forbes list, we could adjust accordingly. For example, the NFL's number 1 over-all pick in the Hefner suite could take a $5 million dollar drop, while the pro skateboarder at Mandalay Bay would fit the $100,000 level. It didn't really matter, because within 3 minutes the deposits would be leveraged and they'd never even know the money was there. So, where in actuality a half a billion dollars was escorted in the back door and then wired to Milan, the financial systems show $5G bar credits to each of our VIPs, as is customary.

We aren't thieves, and honestly what we were doing wasn't even illegal (well, perhaps other than defacing financial security systems and falsifying e-documents). We deposited a surplus, swelling their cash supply by the amount that we needed washed; made the correction by immediately withdrawing the funds, transferring it back out to correct the math; manipulated the system to shrink and launder our load; and then coined it all as an accounting error, a decimal misplacement, or some sort of computer glitch. So, I guess we sort of embody a real life version of Microsoft Money 2.0!

Work subsides and evening approaches. 'Ready' drops me off by Trump Tower for a change of clothes, and as the doorman offered entry I noticed a calla lily arrangement centered in the lobby. I found myself racing to the elevator, urging its rise to top floor suite. My heart hoped to find Vicky, but my spirit prayed for an empty suite.

The door was unlocked…

I slowly pushed forward into the loft and there she was, standing against the window staring out into the desert dusk, accessorized only by Dolce & Gabana from our trip to Milan, and my favorite smile.
"Vicky?!! What, I mean…" Before I could finish, she jumped into my arms, wrapping her body around me so tightly that the only thing I could inhale was her kiss.
"I missed you Alex, I needed to see you!!" As I pulled, and squeezed in response, I became overwhelmed by guilt, acknowledging that I subjected her love to nonsense. Although my lifestyle harvested vacations abroad and extravagant luxuries, the sowing seasons would always spread disappointment in the face of those who aligned themselves with me. But I missed her too, probably more considering the force at which I withdrew myself emotionally. It wasn't safe for her to be in Vegas, not with so much on the line and with so many moving pieces.
"I'm so glad you're here, but how did you…"
Intuition disrupts, and as I begin to reach for my Heckler & Koch tucked away in the base of my spine, a voice from upstairs answers, "I invited her here! Considering it is my fault that you haven't had the time to visit, you know with our little project and all, I felt that it was only fitting that I surprise you with what obviously means the most to you. Consider it a business perk!!" Stepping down the spiral staircase was Anthony Moraino; his face eclipsed by the hustler's smirk and a dark pair of glasses. Irrespective of the risk I was absorbing, he was still positioning power plays; this time using Vicky as insurance against the credits he held on Tripp's life.
"Yeah Alex, he told me that you've been managing his money in something big, and he's had you tied up for the past few months. So, I guess I'm your quarterly bonus!!"

If this were done out of appreciation, perhaps I would have been more gracious. But, he had an angle, and this wasn't just one friend paying for another friend's meal.

"That's right Ace, and after everything closes out tonight, I'll be out of your hair and you can get back to spending time with this beautiful young lady."

My joints tighten as tension erupts throughout my body. The audacity to insert a bystander onto the field of play at this stage of the game just so he could increase capital gains was a destructive tactic. I could see now that this wasn't about a successful venture, his motives had become personal. Why else would he invite my lady the weekend millions of dollars and one of my best friend's lives were at risk?

"Hey, I've got an idea" he smugly continues. "While you finish up the paperwork, why don't I take this lovely young lady to the fight with me and you can meet us there?" Vicky looks to me, uncomfortable at the notion of spending any more time with someone whom she's completely unfamiliar, beyond perhaps a phone convo and plane reservations.

"Well, actually I'd prefer to wait with Alex, seeing as how I haven't seen him in a few months." Suddenly, the front door opens slightly, and two of his goons enter.

"Sir, we're going to be late."

Noticeably, all pleasantries had been extracted from my tone, and were replaced by an infuriation and annoyance similar to what I felt during our South Beach visit. Victoria walks upstairs as Anthony & I step outside of the suite. Once again here we are, face to face for the 3rd time in our history.

"It's your turn slim, to man-up and show what the hell you're made of! Lear Jets, Italian sports cars, Euros, private beaches, foreign exchanges, and ringside seats… Like I've told you before, 'the dice are loaded kid.' Be smart, roll, and cash in while it's hot!"

As he turns to walk away, I find my hand gripping the .45 ACP, lifting it slightly from the tuck under my tee shirt. My finger on the trigger; I could end this game right now! The elevator doors close around him, and I rush back inside to Vicky. My mind was racing in a hundred directions, realizing what I had to do, and what it would cost for me to go through with it. I picked up the phone and call Sykes.

"Joey, we need to run the audible!! Tell Stone and 'Ready' to move on it. Call Tripp, and tell him to hold my seat at the fight, but don't go into detail about anything else. Get 'Quest' & Lola over here ASAP; I need them to stay with Vicky while we finish the job. Make sure you have a conversation with Flow before the fight so he knows exactly what we need done... and I think you know what you need to do too. I'll see you when it's over."

The betting cycle began to fluctuate before finally resting at 3-1 with over $950 million total waged on the strip. At 7:00pm the sports books closed, and we pulled 2 cents from each dollar on the books, giving us a little more than $19 mill in coin interest. This was just to wet the appetite. The real money was to be earned from the fight. I got fitted into Lord & Taylor, and sped over to MGM a few minutes ahead of the Main Event. As I'm walking through the tunnel I see Sykes coming out of Flow's dressing room. He has this cold look on his eyes, something like hate mixed with Decembers in Chicago. He didn't even turn his head to look at me, just walked right passed with the type of cruel intentions that I preferred not to receive directly.

I turned as he approached, "I'm sending the message now." He didn't even nod, just kept walking, unloosing his necktie and tossing it onto the arena basement floor as he disappeared around the corner.

From the tunnel, I could see Tripp and Anthony on the front row. I press 'send' on my PDA and a few moments later Anthony looks to his mobile to review the message. Transferred were the coordinates to where we're going to meet him with wiring instructions to close out the deal. He presses a few buttons, whispers something to Tripp, and tucks his phone back into his jacket pocket. At that exact moment, Flow is lead out of the tunnel towards the cage. The passageway goes dark, and as I lean against the tunnel wall I get this frenzied chill down my spine. He looks at me, and with this weird calm he subtly winks his eye as he begins to bob to a soundtrack of Tupac and crowd boos blasting through the Convention

Center. Cyrus enters the octagon, surrounded by many of his boxing piers and a sea of true MMA fans who just wanted to see him destroyed! The introductions are made, the ring is cleared, and the bell rings for round 1. The fighters circle each other for about 30 seconds, hesitantly searching for weaknesses and points of attack. But neither flinches, and as they begin to settle down and move towards the middle of the ring. Just then, 'Ready' calls me on my mobile. He was outside of the convention center monitoring the casino floor and hotel perimeter.

"Ace, I just saw Agent Lugar jet through the lobby and out of the building!! I heard him shout to his partner something about "a tip" he received. He just left him and went solo! There's no way for us to follow him without being obvious. What should we do?"

"Don't bother following him; we know where he's going. Have everyone get in position at the spot so we can close the books on this job."

Then it happened…

The kid throws a sloppy straight kick and Cyrus catches him square on the chin with a 1, 2, combination that puts him to sleep before his back even touches the canvas! His head smashes the mat so violently that it jars his eyes open while the rest of his body lay motionless, twisted against the side of the cage steel like a car wreck!!

Amidst the chaos and boos, I receive a text from Sykes: "I spoke with 'Ready.' I'm in position, and should be done in about 20 minutes." In Flow's exuberant celebration, he climbs to the top of the cage, on the side closest to where Tripp and Anthony were sitting. He stares at Tripp with a fierceness that suggests "You're next," and then winks his eye as he exits into the tunnel. Moraino tries to hide his disgust, pulling down his shades in an effort to conceal his disproval. He pulls out his mobile once again, violently begins to text what I'm sure are lots of four letter words, and storms toward the exit, while Tripp follows with a confused and unrelenting look on his face.

As I fade into the tunnel exit, I called 'Ready.'

"They're coming your way. Make sure they've got transportation."
Before I could even hang up, Sykes dials-in on the other line.
"Ace, he's here. He can't see me... I'm ducked beside the abandoned building..."
I could hear footsteps, followed by another voice, apparently on the phone.
"Boss, I'm here. I see an old building and a Porsche parked with the headlamps burning. Give me 10 minutes to look around and I'll call you back."
Then, "FREEZE!!!"
A few seconds later, a shotgun blast pierces through my Bluetooth like a Molotov Cocktail!!
"Ace, he's hit! I think I blew both of his legs off!! Give me 15 minutes, and I'll meet you on the strip!" As he tries to disconnect from the call, I could hear the terrifying screams of anguish through his mobile tuner. The cries get louder and louder as Sykes approaches the suffering & apparently dismembered body.
"Good evening Agent Lugar. I guess we know who Anthony Moraino has been texting all freakin' night!!!"

I could here Sykes kick away his gun, as well as what sounded like detached limbs and shoes. "Perhaps we should become better acquainted. I'd like to introduce myself. I... I... am my father's son, a second generation Vegas hustler. You knew my father... about 15 years ago? As a matter of fact, you bragged to Ace about meeting him. You don't remember? Think really... really, hard!! Here's a hint: You'd probably remember him as......... "RATTLESNAKE VENUM, and SHOTGUN SHELLS!!"

Complete silence.

"Let's talk..."

[Click]

....

"Ace, you know that I love you like a brother, right?"

Chapter 16: Laser-Guided Escrow //

"Ok 'Ready,' it's on you now! Make sure that Tripp and Anthony get to the location so we can finish the job."
Here I am, shuffling through the backstage VIP entrance, trying to escape the FBI and delusional gangsters who do not yet see the beauty in my work. In a 12 hour workday, I infiltrated the casino financial systems, laundered $500 million cash, stripped $19 million in pennies from the betting public, flipped a third of over $400 million on Mixed Martial Arts, unfortunately became a potential accessory to murder, and there was still the issue of moving the bills out of the US before sun-up Eastern Standard Time.

Stone paid Moraino's driver to take he and Tripp to a private airstrip, west of McCarran International. From a wireless bug inside the Benz, I could hear Anthony questioning the location, screaming how I'd given him coordinates to a previous drop spot. Consider it a favor. From what I heard via Bluetooth, it was in his best interest not to venture south into the empty desert where Sykes was determined to "break even."

I called Vicky… there was no answer. Lola & 'Quest' weren't answering their phones either. Stone and 'Ready' picked me up behind the Mirage, and we headed south on the boulevard towards McCarran. I kept calling, and still there is no answer. We detoured east back to Trump International to find her. My suite was empty, and there weren't any signs of struggle. Not even a martini glass was out of place. I'd only been gone for an hour or so, but something just wasn't sitting right with this whole thing. The girls wouldn't leave without telling me, and 'Quest' wasn't some little push over who'd go down without a fight. This was exactly why I didn't want her here, but as concerned as I was, I had to trust that they were able to handle themselves, and focus on finishing out the job before I lost control of my emotions. We pull onto a side street, just south of the rear quarter entrance of the airstrip. Then the phone rings…

"Victoria?!!"

"No, it's Sykes. I'm on my way to the setup spot, but I have to drop something off first." My eardrum vibrates at the soundtrack of Agent Lugar's hellacious screams and the vibrato hissing of rattlesnakes. "I was 15 years old when the morgue unzipped that bag, revealing my father's punctured face and torn remains. His skin was green and swollen from hundreds of snake injections, not to mention his limbs were in a separate Ziploc due to multiple shotgun blasts that ripped him in two." I could here Sykes stomping away at what must have been a motionless cadaver, kept alive only through conversation. Son, I'm sorry! I never meant to hurt your father." I couldn't bear to listen, and even as I screamed for Sykes to stop, I couldn't hang up the phone. It was as if he needed someone to help his conscious settle with whatever decision he was about to make. Emotionally, I couldn't allow him to carry this burden around on his own, like the rusted slug from his father's heart he carried in his pocket.

"You told Alex that "15 years ago, some young punk thought he could run the strip without asking for your permission," and that "you'd hate to have to reload 12 gauges and revisit the rattlesnake ranch!!" The hissing gets louder and louder. "No need to revisit the ranch, I already did!" A thud as the sack of snakes is dropped onto the cold desert floor beside Agent Lugar's beaten, dismembered body. Engine revs, and the screams fade amidst screeching tires and Led Zeppelin blasting through sand & humidity. The Soundtrack to his madness is interrupted by sniffles and his whimpering voice. "I'll be there in 5 minutes guys... Alex put me on speaker, because there's something all of you need to know..."

A few minutes later we pull onto the landing strip, some 5 miles of concrete where no one would interrupt our business. The benediction of our professional dealings would be delivered here, and we all could transition into the private sector of taxes and bank issued checkbooks. Anthony, his enforcers, and Tripp were already waiting. Stone, 'Ready,'

and I pull up slowly, surveying the landscape for anything out of place.
Jayda & Koryn emerge from the opposite side of the building, having
patrolled the area… they're fitted with AKs, and of course the dogs. They
gave the nod that everything was clean, and backed away where their aim
would be best served. Anthony opens his stance and walks toward me.
"Who the hell do you think you are, huh? WHERE'S THE MONEY?
How much did we win or lose? Why did you change the location?"
This is exactly why I don't do business in person, and why I only allow
one face-to-face per client. If you give them too much personal time, they
feel that they can get away with anything.
"You've got some balls thinking you control the terms here!! You crossed
the line when you comp'd my ladies flight in the middle of our business.
We cleaned a half a bill for your in one day, gained you an extra $19M
just from pinching crumbs, and capped $166 million from a freakin' cage
fight! All of the money I made you today, and got the nerve to question
me?!"

    "Because that's not what we agreed to ALEX! I needed the fight
money flipped on the "under," which would have turned $400 into 1.2
B's, and you were supposed to have guaranteed that. So, we aren't
leaving unless we salvage our business."
I stepped directly to his face, "We're done!!! You walk away with about
$685 million, plus $65M from us to cover Tripp's business line. You can
keep our cut… and don't worry about the real estate flip you promised; we
don't need it! I'll wire the money out to your boys right now, and once
it's received, we're closing the books."

    "I don't think so Alex. You see, I need more than $700 mill &
some change to buy and tend to my powder project in Columbia. So, I'm
not leaving here without severance pay!" He walks over to a parked SUV,
lifts the hatchback, and pulls Vicky out by her hair. He pushes her onto
her hands and knees, as her evening wear rips in response.
"I'd hate to have to settle my debt via your pretty little girl friend here!!"

    I begin to reach for my divider, but it would do little good with
Vicky standing between us. I could here Jayda release the safety clip, but

I reached my hand out to her in a gesture to relax. "So Alex, you've got the power to make it right!" He snatches Vicky to her feet by her hair, holding a gun to her neck. "I'm gonna need you to wire the $685M, plus an addition $300M of your own to even out the score. If you don't, I'm gonna blow her spine through the front of her rib cage! You've got uhm… 45 seconds!!"

Suddenly, police sirens and red lights lace the highway, bringing the boulevard lightshow to the airstrip.
"Anthony, the police are on their way man. You can't intimidate us with guns and think you…"
Interrupting, "EITHER YOU DO IT," calling up a hollow point to the chamber, "OR I'M GONNA PUT STEEL INTO THE BACK OF HER HEAD!! WIRE THE DAMN MONEY BOY!!" I snatch the laptop from the back seat and began the wiring process. The instructions were already designated; I just needed to insert the password.
"Anthony, after I insert the transfer code, the money's yours. But first, send Vicky over here to punch it in!" I step away from the computer.
"Send her over there to put in the password in; that's the only way we can do this! Let her type it in, or I'll make sure that your $900 million deposit is spread out over 50 years!!" He releases her and she slowly walks over to the car hood. "The password is our gift, yours, mine, and your father's gift. Just type it in and press ENTER."

I don't think I'll ever forget the look in her eyes. It wasn't fear, it was disappointment that I'd allowed her to be placed in harms way. With all that I'd wanted for us, this life that I live destroyed any hope of the kind of love that we both deserved. "You know the password baby; it's in the lobby…just type it in, and press ENTER!" She types "Calla Lillie" and the transferal process starts.

"She did it! Check it!" Anthony gestures to Tripp to confirm receipt of funds with his financial people.
"Is it good? OK!! Anthony, they said its showing up."
The horns from the police sirens trigger nerves that instinctively force everyone to pull guns. Suddenly, Tripp steps in the middle of everything.

"EVERYBODY LOWER YOUR PIECES! Fellas, we can make this real simple…" He pleads with Moraino to put the gun down… Anthony reluctantly hands his pistol over to Tripp, though no one else lowers their weapons.

Tripp takes a deep breath.
With his back turned, to me he screams out, "Ace, you know that I love you like a brother, right?"
I push Vicky over to 'Ready,' "I know Jeremy, but…"
He suddenly turns; stepping in front of Moraino, and lifts the barrel point in my direction.

        "But we're not brothers! And, so like you were told several years ago: "…it's your turn Pryce, to man up and show what the hell you're made of!!!"

• • • • • • • • • • •

"Per your request..."

Chapter 17: "Allure" & Oasis //

"TRIPP, WHAT THE HELL ARE YOU DOIN' MAN?!!"

"I'm taking my place Alex. I chose sides a long time ago… don't look so surprised!"

"Tripp, what the…"

"What am I doing? What the hell have you been doing Alex? You've enjoyed success at my feet for years and never showed me any gratitude!! All of you! When Moraino first introduced himself to you, we were transferring control of all of his businesses to me. I tried to put you on by sending you some work. You remember when you were trying to squeeze pennies from IRAs and Trust Funds? But he had to stay on as a cover when you lost your nerve and decided to exit out! I knew I couldn't come to you and expect you to accept the fact that I got connected on my own. I had to hide the truth about Miami for your own protection… and did you ever thank me? How do you think Moraino got your card all those years ago? Who do you think sent him North to your minor league chop-shop office in Chicago? You were an average broker before us! I MADE YOU INTO WHO YOU ARE TODAY!! I blessed you with a glorified lottery ticket, bought the SEC so you wouldn't get caught, and hired the guns to protect you if questions were raised. Who do you think sent 'Ready' on jobs and connected into Stone's office at the Commission? Did you really think it was coincidence that I came across you at Harvard? Come on Ace, you're smarter than that! All of this time, I was the one who was leading the way, and you were just mid-level management!!"

"Tripp, who cares about any of that? We've made millions of dollars and live a lifestyle that 99% of the world can't relate to! Having $500 mill that you never have to pay taxes on is better than having a billion that you do! Who cares about…?"

"I CARE!! You were off on your little boat with your slouch while I was bringing in the money. Sykes is the Vegas celebrity, Stone is the glue, 'Ready' is the muscle… But what about me? I had to blackmail you just so you'd show me some compassion… and what do you do? You screw me!?"

"I SCREWED YOU!? I guess it's a coincidence that Victoria is here, huh? The job wouldn't have gone down this way had you not placed her in harm. You brought this on yourself…"

The sirens get louder, and red lights become visibly brighter in the distance. All of those years of hard work, aggressive practices of discretion, sweeping away the digital trail, and living above the law have finally caught up with us. I stare into Tripp's eyes; but this time there's no poker face, no laughter, no hopes of reconnecting with my friend who'd toast vodka shots under high beams & Hip-Hop.

"I love you Ace… but this is business. I decided a long time ago that I wouldn't put friendships above power!!" Tripp turns the handgun across his chest and points in the direction of Victoria. "But, I'm not sorry for what I've gotta do…"

Unexpectedly, Jayda & Koryn both initiate warfare, tapping Moraino and his crew in the chest with rapid fire. Tripp turns and hesitates, at which moment I knock the piece from his hand, reaching for the Heckler I kept creased in my belt. Shots let out, and 'Ready' is able to get Victoria into the car and as Stone speeds away from the airstrip. "I'm not sorry either Tripp…" Dead bodies and tire smoke engage, and I can almost feel the police headlamps bearing down on me. With my left hand, I point the .45 into his eye socket, opposite palm pressed to his throat to ensure fatal accuracy.

"Freeze Alex, FBI! DROP THE WEAPON!!!" It's the same young FBI agent from the restaurant, Agent Lugar's boy whose name… I don't know. I hesitate. I consider accepting life in prison in exchange for his death, to ensure that the fairest form of justice is carried out. He was a pariah, my former best friend who had become the world's most dangerous purveyor of criminal activity. If I let him up, he'd coast through the legal system and get away without any penalty of law.

"WE WILL NOT WARN YOU AGAIN! DROP YOUR WEAPON ALEX!!" He looks up at me from his back, as I grip death in one hand and his voice box in the other.
"NOW ALEX; OR WE WILL OPEN FIRE!!"

I close my eyes and squeeze…

…But not hard enough. I release my fire arm to the officer and am slammed into the concrete.

Handcuffed and in the back of a police car, I watch as Tripp fabricates his way into an approaching Maybach, identical to the one that picked he and Moraino up from the casino. The Federal Agent sits in the front passenger seat of the patrol car, and turns to me with a blank look. Again, he has no real expression on his face, just eyes that seep a weird sort of apathy. I wondered who he felt sorry for… but I knew.
"Six dead bodies, no motive, attempted murder, trespassing; sounds like one hell of a Saturday night Ace!"

Even as the Benz disappears around the corner, likely headed East on 593 towards Hoover, I'm regretting not trusting my catalytic instincts, closing both of our eyes forever in what would have been the most honest thing we've shared in a long time. For what I'd done in my life, I did not particularly deserve mercy from the court system…. nor did Tripp deserve mercy from me!!

He rides along the highway, luxury curtains closed, arrogance seeping through the exhaust of his six figure get away car. The phone rings, and it's his bankers.
"Tripp, the money is being moved out! I mean, it's just vanishing right on the screen!! I don't know what's going on…"

In a panicky response, he tears through his computer keys, logging into his personal financial system to witness as all $985 million is being counted down to zero like Dick Clark's "Rockin' Eve!!" Furious, he calls Agent Lugar. Everyone else on his Vegas payroll had been left for dead at the tarmac. He here's a synchronized cell phone ringing inside of the Benz.

"Lugar?" Suddenly, the car stops.

"What are we stopping for?! Where am I? C.J., is that you?"

He widens the side view curtains to reveal darkness wrapped around an abandoned structure, and Agent Lugar's car parked in the front.

"Where are we?"

He tries to get out, but the doors are locked.

"What the…"

An intro of guitar blasts through BOSE speakers, interrupting his fearful interrogation by way of his requested LP.

"Today is gonna be the day that they're gonna throw it back to you!"

Screaming at the driver, "WHO THE HELL ARE YOU? DO YOU KNOW WHO I AM?!"

"By now you should've somehow realized what you've got to do!"

Ironic, how Oasis would accompany Tripp through his failed attempt into safe haven. A steady calm begins to rest over his expression, almost in acceptance to inevitability.

There's a bottle of our favorite house liquor, and a note:

Per your request, & as promised, 'Wonderwall' to the person who leaves first… And a bottle of house liquor to smooth out your travels. Save room for the rest of us Jeremy, we'll all be together again… in the mean time, work on your poker face.

-Ace

The hustler's smirk creeps across his face, followed by a somber moment of acceptance. The Maybach partition screen retreat as he continues to mouth the words of his favorite recording. Lola and 'Quest' reveal themselves in the front seat; faces bloodied and battered, haven been attacked during Vicky's abduction earlier in the night. He takes back a double shot straight from the bottle, as tears and vodka stream down his chin.

"I don't believe that anybody…"

"WONDERWALL… I have to admit Ace, it was a nice touch!"

"…feels the way I do, about you NOW!!"

Lifting his tearful expression and the bottle towards the Nevada hills, he manages a whisper: "Cheers……… Brother!"

Lola turns and opens fire into the cabin area, as the back seat transforms into a Cirque du Soleil performance with a violent display of physical contortionism & laser firing optics, courtesy of Crimson Trace.

Gun shots blow through the distant breeze; synchronized with effects from the "Allure" we promised to interject into his funeral ceremony. As one track interludes death, the other drowns our guilt. The question I asked before we took on this job was: *"Is any of this really worth it?"* And though he didn't answer, I have to believe that his heart wanted to whisper "No." From obliging Tripp's request to play this song at his funeral, to once again resting upon my refuge at the western rim of Hoover Dam, that moment for both of us was an oasis. It's been weeks, and I still haven't stopped mourning. I can't shake these memories, like the walk through the Harvard courtyard, Friday nights in 'Freedom,' and his bad poker face. He was my friend; but I guess there are no friends in this business. And as much as I need to erase him from my memory, the song keeps playing in my mind. "Wonderwall," just as the brick sanctuary of Hoover has once again become my "wonder wall." Jeremy will always be a part of who I am… I just wish we would have figured out how to save each other before it was too late.

The arresting agent and his comrades, who perhaps played the biggest part in this job, haven't surfaced above their guilt since they watched Agent Lugar speed away from an MGM entrance. There was a reason why I never mentioned his name… it was because he never told me. He didn't want to be associated with the downfall of a fellow agent, but instead wanted to surrender into a private life of wealth beyond the Vegas strip & the bureau's crooked history. In pleading for his life, Agent Lugar told Sykes that Jeremy was the mastermind behind everything. And so $600 million is split only four ways; a down payment on reaching longevity in justifiable markets with accounts that pay real taxes. $85M made our girls, agents, side kicks, brokers, and associates happy to fade away. These days my Friday reservations are wherever Victoria chooses. 'Freedom' is no longer a treble filled night club, but instead a loft along the French Riviera with full view of the Mediterranean.

Suddenly, my pocket pulsates in response to an incoming call; only fitting that a female voice breaks through Bluetooth silence. I don't think I'll ever forget that phone call…

"So… I hear you're the new player! I've gotta admit, I like the way you & your crew do business. Personally, I never liked Anthony or Tripp; they didn't understand how the game works… but I guess you know that. Issue is, we still have 20 acres for sale in Columbia and no lineup. I understand moving blow isn't your biz, but my boss is looking to work something out. We're alike you and me; I got into the game by running numbers through Panama & Venezuela, back when Miami was popular. No one has struck gold in the US since the late 90's, and we're looking to fill that lane. We'll triple your revenue for helping introduce our digits into the US marketplace. The word is you're retired… Well, I guess we'll have to just wait and see! One of my associates will present themselves to you in the near future. What happens then is up to you… Ciao!"

[Click]

It appears that the Vegas strip has "*reintroduced* me to the 'at-all-costs' lifestyle I've acceded to." The dew finds me at Hoover Dam, resting upon its rim searching for something other than historical perspective. An anonymous phone call was an invitation to the big boys table. And as I encase myself in foreign engineering, the speedometer seems to offer the clearest answer. Speeding, hardly recognizing the danger at which I was traveling, served as a synonym for what my subconscious was quickly suggesting. From Las Vegas fight nights, to speed boats on Dade County shores, to the industrial plains of Medellin.........

"I'm in my Zone!!"

To be continued...

Bibliography, Citation Acknowledgements, & Points of Reference //

Photographic images courtesy of ©iStockPhoto.com/illustrious

Jay-Z. "American Dreamin'." American Gangster.
    Island Def Jam, Roc-A-Fella, 2007.

Jay-Z. "Dead Presidents II." Reasonable Doubt.
    Roc-A-Fella, 1996.

Jackson, Michael. "Don't Stop 'til You Get Enough."
    Off the Wall. Epic Records, 1979.

Nas. "It ain't hard to tell." Illmatic. Columbia, 1994.

Prince. "Adore." Sign 'O' the Times. Paisley Park, 1987.

Oasis. "Wonderwall." (What's the Story) Morning Glory?.
    Creation Records, 1995.

Jay-Z. "Allure." The Black Album. Roc-A-Fella, 2003.

Frank Sinatra. "The girl from Ipanema." Francis Albert Sinatra
    & Antonio Carlos Jobim. Reprise Records, 1967.

Frank Sinatra with Bill May. "It had to be you." Trilogy.
    Reprise Records, 1979.

A Raisin in the Sun. Dr. Daniel Petrie. Columbia Pictures,
    1961.

The Bourne Supremacy. Dir. Paul Greengrass.
    Universal Studios, 2004.

Boiler Room. Dir. Ben Younger. New Line Cinema, 2000.

Wall Street. Dir. Oliver Stone. 20th Century Fox, 1987.

Miami Vice. Executive Producer Michael Mann. NBC,
    1984-1989.

The Cosby Show. Created by Ed Weinberger, Michael J.
    Leeson, & William Cosby Jr. Ed.D. Carsey-Werner
    NBC, 1984-1992.

The Andy Griffith Show. Created by Sheldon Leonard. CBS,
    1960-1968.

American Gangster. Dir. Ridley Scott. Universal Pictures,
    2007.

Pirates of the Caribbean. Dir. Gore Verbinski. Walt Disney
    Pictures, 2003.

Batman. Warner Brothers, 1989-Present.

New Jack City. Dir. Mario Van Peebles. Warner Brothers,
    1991.

Carlito's Way. Dir. Brian de Palma. Universal Pictures, 1993.

The Holy Bible: New Testament. Luke 21:37-22:6, KJV.

The Holy Bible: Old Testament. Daniel 6:1-22, KJV.

Also by T.J. Breeden

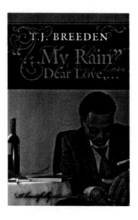

"In putting this book together, my process was to create a collection of verses that would tell a story, making it effortless to enjoy and at the same time inviting you, the reader, into a temporary state of emotional being. Successfully doing so has made this book innovatively unique, in that it is a biography, letter, diary, script, and novel, all disguised as poetry. It represents a state of physical, spiritual, and rational sensation, beginning as a description of romantic innocence, and evolves to demonstrate levels of social consciousness, spirituality, physical expression, disappointment, misunderstanding, passionate reconnection, and finally the "credits roll" in light of an epiphany: "Dear Love,...""

"...My Rain" *Dear Love,...*
"A beautifully articulated poetic journey..."
T.J. Breeden

ISBN: 1-4241-7844-4

Available from PublishAmerica, wherever books are sold.
www.publishamerica.com
www.myrain.info

The Lion's Den

Chronicles of a Las Vegas Money Launderer

THE LION'S DEN | CHRONICLES OF A LAS VEGAS MONEY LAUNDERER. A NOVEL BY T.J. BREEDEN. IN ASSOCIATION WITH THE lbL MEDIA GROUP. STARRING ALEX "ACE" PRYCE, JOEY SYKES, KYLE STONE, JEREMY "TRIPP" STARR, 'READY,' AND ANTHONY MORAINO

lbL Media Group

THE LION'S DEN. COPYRIGHT © T.J. BREEEDEN. ALL RIGHTS RESERVED.